INTERESTING FACTS ABOUT THE STATE OF ARIZONA

For Joanne, of course,
and for my parents,
Kenneth and Janet Poolman

Interesting Facts
About the State of Arizona

JEREMY POOLMAN

faber and faber
LONDON · BOSTON

First published in Great Britain in 1996
by Faber and Faber Limited
3 Queen Square London WC1N 3AU

Phototypeset by Datix International Ltd, Bungay, Suffolk
Printed and bound in Great Britain by
Mackays of Chatham PLC, Chatham, Kent

© Jeremy Poolman, 1996

Jeremy Poolman is hereby identified as author of this work
in accordance with Section 77 of the Copyright,
Designs and Patents Act 1988.

A CIP record for this book is available from the British Library

ISBN 0-571-17614-3

2 4 6 8 10 9 7 5 3 1

One

THE FOLLOWING, from the *Bagdad Bugle*, reprinted from *Elevator News*, journal of the Elevator Association of America:

> It is with regret that the death is announced of Ethan Pierce, 91, former south-western representative of Bell-Boy Elevators Inc., Chicago, Ill. May all who have risen find peace.
>
> (Matthew, 1:iv).

'I never knew that,' said Virginia. 'Did you know that?' She was standing at the counter of the Bagdad General Store, perusing the pages of a newspaper.

'Know what?'

'About Ethan.'

Dorothy Brinkman lifted her eyes from their study of a can of corned beef. 'What?'

'About him being in elevators.'

She sighed and returned her gaze to the can. *Produce*, she read, *of Argentina*. She replaced the can on the shelf. Argentina, she knew, had a very bad record and was not to be encouraged by trade.

'Well, did you?'

'Did I what?'

'Know that about Ethan?'

Wearily she let her eyes drift along the shelf. Outside on Main Street one of the Jemson boys — Perry or Philly, she couldn't make out which — was sitting on the running-board of his pick-up, smoking a cigarette.

'I was asking you a question, Dorothy.'

'I know you were, Virginia.'

'So?'

She narrowed her eyes. Perry it was who had the scar. Or was it Philly? She couldn't remember. She turned away, back into the store. 'I don't know what you're talking about,' she said.

'I'm *talking* about Ethan.'

'Well, I wish you wouldn't.'

'Why not?'

'It's morbid, that's why.'

'No it's not.'

'It *is* to go *on* so.'

'I'm seventy-eight,' said Virginia decisively. 'I can do what I like.'

Dorothy sighed and shook her head. Ethan, Ethan. Ever since news had reached them of the discovery of the body, Virginia had talked of little else. 'People should be ashamed,' she'd informed her sister several times during breakfast that morning and again on their way to the store, 'leaving an old man alone like that.' It was, she'd said as they'd watched Father Raoul drive by in his Datsun, a disgrace. Father Raoul, sensing their attention, had turned and waved and Dorothy had waved back. Virginia, however, had not. It wasn't right, she'd said, levity from a Mexican in the face of death.

'And anyway,' said Virginia, 'I don't know what you're so cool about. He was *your* boyfriend.'

'Oh, don't be ridiculous!'

She shrugged. 'Everyone says so.'

'*You* say so, you mean.'

Virginia turned the page of the paper, casual-like.

Dorothy looked away. Outside in the street the Jemson boy was twisting his heel on the butt of a cigarette. She studied the scar on his cheek. Not waving to Father Raoul had been a discourtesy: another example of her sister's increasing rudeness. 'You must apologize,' she said coolly.

'Apologize?'

'To Father Raoul. You were extremely rude, ignoring him like that.'

'Will not!'

'Then I shall have to for you.'

4

'You'll do no such thing!'

'I shall have to.'

'Nonsense! If lover-boy wants to go around laughing and joking while his flock are dropping like flies –' Virginia dropped her voice at the sound of a screen-door banging. 'Well,' she hissed, 'that's *his* affair. Just don't expect me to join in!'

'Morning, ladies.'

'Morning, Frank,' said Dorothy.

Frank Tyler laid a box of frozen kippers on the counter. 'You alright, Ginny?'

Virginia shrugged.

'Your sister been giving you a hard time?' He winked at Dorothy. Together they looked at Virginia. Virginia was blushing.

'We were talking about Ethan,' she said. 'At least I was.'

'Ah yes,' said Frank.

'Dorothy thinks we should forget it. What happened, I mean. I mean him being left alone an' all –'

'That's not what I said.'

'Is.'

'It certainly was a bad one,' said Frank. He lifted the box of kippers and carried it to the freezer. 'Still, things must go on, I guess.'

'Exactly,' said Dorothy. She smiled at Virginia. Unseen by Frank Tyler, Virginia stuck out her tongue.

'You ladies be there for the party?' Frank turned away from the freezer, he was frowning. 'Should I call it a party?'

'It's a look-see,' said Virginia.

'It's called a wake, Virginia,' said Dorothy. 'You know very well it is. A chance for folks to pay their respects.'

'To gawp, you mean.'

'I mean, to pay their respects. It's what people do.'

Virginia huffed.

Frank closed the freezer. The ice inside hissed. 'Anyway, ladies, you'll be there, I take it?' He warmed his hands on his thighs. 'He'd have wanted you there, I'm sure. You being his friends an' all.'

'We'll be there,' said Dorothy.

'Maybe,' said Virginia. 'Maybe not.'

In the corner the freezer clicked and hummed.

It was sweltering in the street, the heat shimmering off the dusty sidewalk. Virginia wandered off across the street towards Reno's. Dorothy paused for a moment in the shade of the store, struggling with her parasol. From the corner of her eye she could see the Jemson boy watching.

'Having trouble?' he said.

Dorothy shrugged. 'Oh it's just old, that's all,' she said, nearly adding, *like me.*

The pick-up's springs creaked as the boy stood up. His boots crunched across the sidewalk. In his rough hands the parasol looked tiny, like a child's umbrella. In a moment it was up. The boy handed it back. He smiled and the scar on his cheek buckled.

'I should get it fixed.'

The boy shrugged, still smiling.

It's Perry, thought Dorothy. She smiled at his sun-browned face. 'Anyway, I'm obliged,' she said. Then she turned and made her way across the street, imagining as she did so eyes following her.

It was close in Reno's despite the efforts of two whirring fans on the wall behind the bar. Dorothy ordered iced tea and sat down.

'What did *he* want?' said Virginia.

'Who?'

'Lover-boy.'

Dorothy gazed, nonchalant, about the bar. The old pool table was deserted, cues standing idle in their racks. 'I don't know who you mean,' she said.

'Yes you do. Philly Jemson.'

'It wasn't Philly Jemson.'

'Was.'

'It was Perry.'

'Was not.'

'Was so.'

Pointedly, Virginia sucked the last of her Coke through a straw. 'We'll ask,' she said.

A man of slight build but with a curiously large head (a condition for which too much thinking had never been blamed), Reno Stuckey set Dorothy's iced tea on the table and peered through the glass panel in the door. 'Yep, that's Philly all right,' he said.

'See!'

'No way that could be Perry.'

Virginia smiled triumphant. '*She* thought so.'

'Nah, couldn't be. Perry's in Phoenix. Some job, he said. Won't be back till tomorrow, he said. Hey, you girls want the Big O?'

Flushed with her victory Virginia said okay, she was beaming. In a moment the voice of Roy Orbison filled the air:

> *I'm goin' back someday*
> *Gonna stay*
> *On Blue Bayou*

It was after eleven when they left Reno's. Main Street was deserted, the heat of the desert lying heavy and still. Virginia strolled ahead, out past Big Bill's Auto Repairs and the boarded-up Belle vue Motel, her cotton dress hanging down from the bones of her shoulders. She gazed into the front yards of houses. At least half of the houses now were closed up, the yards abandoned, families driven out to the city by the times. She peered into mail-boxes, empty now. She strolled on, her heels raising dust.

Dorothy caught up with her outside the old Nichols' place. Virginia was shading her eyes.

'What are you doing?' said Dorothy.

'Just looking.'

They walked on together in silence. They turned on Constitution. Virginia paused.

'What is it now?'

'I was thinking,' she said. 'About Ethan's boy.'

Dorothy sighed.

'Do you think we shall like him?'

7

'What?'

Virginia shrugged. 'I was just wondering, that's all.'

Dorothy shook her head and walked on. Ethan, Ethan. She crossed the street briskly, heading for home. Sometimes she wished she'd never heard of Ethan Pierce.

FRANK TYLER CLOSED the store as usual at noon. Ordinarily he'd have crossed the street to Reno's for a beer and a game of pool, but not today. Today, he selected a can of paint from the shelves in the storeroom and made his way through to the yard. He pulled on his baseball cap. He sat for a moment behind the wheel of his pick-up, thinking gloomily of the task ahead.

He listened to the radio as he drove out of town, losing the Flagstaff stations and picking up those from Phoenix as he headed south-east towards the highway. *It's never easy letting go,* sang a sweet southern girl. Frank Tyler tapped his silver ring on the wheel.

In all of the fifty-three years that had passed since Franklin Delano Tyler had entered the world as a squalling pink-skinned bundle of joy, the town of Bagdad had never not been in a state of decline. Once the jewel of Bill Williams County, it had given its sons for the nation's wars and then to the nation's cities. Young men and women whose grandparents could still remember first sighting Arizona's great plains, and the mountains beyond and the vast empty steel-blue sky, had left in search of better lives elsewhere in Phoenix or Los Angeles or Chicago or New York, and fewer and fewer had ever returned. In time the town had dwindled. Now, in his fifty-fourth year, Frank Tyler knew it was dying.

He pulled off onto the dirt and cut the engine.

As a boy, young Frankie had stood on a box in the window of his father's general store watching the comings and goings at the Bellevue Motel – the gamblers' sleek cars on their way to Las Vegas, the couples from the east fleeing west to get married – and he'd thought it all certain to endure. It would grow, he'd thought then, as he grew, spreading out like the houses on Constitution Drive, devouring the desert mile after mile like some fiendish machine. He'd stood in the crowds on the fourth of July, sure that nothing would ever change, unaware that even while he was watching it was changing, and not for the better. As the band passed by, batons twirling, drums thumping, he could scarcely have guessed that even then the town was doomed. By the time he was twenty the Bellevue was failing, starved by the Interstate of the gamblers and their cars; by his thirtieth birthday it was closed. That summer, while the rest of America was tearing itself apart, he'd stood on the sidewalk outside Forbes Electrical watching American soldiers giving V-signs in a jungle, amazed by the way things were going.

The engine ticked as it cooled. He sat for a while just gazing at the highway as memories of that summer drew up like a tide, then receded. The highway was empty, shimmering in the heat. From here, on a clear day, you could see Aquila and Wenden and the tiny glinting cars out on Interstate Ten. On a clear day like today you could see half of Arizona — the vast flat dung-colored desert and beyond that the mountains and beyond them the huge western sky. It was days like today that made America seem endless, still a land of opportunity, a land with the power still to inspire a man's dreams, a land still fertile beyond imagination, still seething with life, still beckoning. For Frank Tyler even now such a day, such a sight, still took his breath away as it had when he'd stood there as a boy. Even now it still filled his heart with the future's possibilities and stirred for a moment in his old blood the hope of his youth.

But only for a moment.

He opened the door of his pick-up and stood in the fierce noon sun, tugging on the peak of his Sun-Devils cap. Optimism these days was fleeting, always draining away like water through cupped hands. Lately, he'd taken to standing in his yard late at night just listening to the whispering of the desert, waiting for — what? Someone? Something? He'd lie still in his bed thinking more and more of the past, hearing nothing in the darkness but the hissing of cars far off on the Interstate and the hum of the power in the lines.

He lifted his cap and wiped his forehead with the back of his hand. A rust-colored lizard scuttled past in the dust. He replaced the cap, pulling it down. He removed his things from the back of the pick-up. He trudged across the road and set to work.

It was hard painting in the sun but he got it done and when he was through he stepped back to check on his work. *Bagdad,* he read, *Pop. 312.* The number was wet and one less than yesterday. Always one less, he thought gloomily.

He listened to the radio as he drove back to town, losing the Phoenix stations and picking up those from Flagstaff. *Come to Cooper's* said a man. He switched the radio off. He drove the rest of the way in silence.

Some nights Frank Tyler had a dream. He dreamed he woke to find the town completely gone — blown away back to sand by the warm desert wind.

3

THEY WERE STANDING that evening at the lights on the corner of Main and Constitution.

'Well?'

'Well what?'

'Are you going to do it?'

Virginia shrugged. 'I might.'

'Might?'

'Or I might not. Anyhow, I don't see as it matters.'

'It matters to me.'

The lights flicked to red, halting invisible traffic. Dorothy lifted her basket of sandwiches and set off. Virginia followed, scuffing her sneakers in the dust.

'Dorothy?'

'What?'

'Do you think he'll really come?'

'Who?'

'Ethan's boy.'

Dorothy strode on, heels clipping, saying nothing.

'Dorothy?'

She changed the basket hand to hand.

'Will he be naked do you think? Ethan I mean, in his coffin –'

Dorothy stopped abruptly and turned. Her arms were aching from the weight of the basket. 'Look,' she said sharply, 'I don't know why you insist on going on like this, but whyever it is I wish you'd stop. Heavens, I only asked you to apologize –'

Virginia shrugged. 'I was only wondering –'

'Well, don't!'

Dorothy turned and walked on. Behind her, Virginia stuck out her tongue.

They passed along Constitution, through lengthening shadows, out beyond the reach of the street-lights. Bats flew, clipping the dusk. In the distance the mountains were dark and huge.

There were lights on in the Pierce house, a shaft of yellow stretching out across the yard. Father Raoul's Datsun was parked in the street. Behind it was an out-of-state Chevy.

'Promise me,' said Dorothy. They were standing on the path.

'Promise you what?'

'You know very well what. That you'll say you're sorry.'

Virginia bit her lip, considering. She studied the light in the front-room window. The window was ajar, the room empty.

'Well?'

'Well what?'

'Promise me.'

Virginia shrugged. She crossed her fingers behind her and promised.

He was dressed in his Sunday suit, white shirt, dark tie. His eyes were closed, his face pale. On his lips there was a trace of rouge.

'Spooky,' said Virginia, peering into the coffin. An elbow dug her sharply in the ribs.

'Ssh.'

'Why?'

'Just ssh.'

Virginia shrugged.

Dorothy looked about the room. It was different from the room she remembered. The chairs had been moved back against the walls as if for a dance, and there were flowers in a vase on the mantle. The coffin had been set on a table beneath the open window. The air in the room was sweet with night-jasmine.

'Dorothy?'

'What now?'

'I was wondering.'

Dorothy sighed. 'What?'

'Well, you know how he couldn't smell things?'

13

'Yes – so?'

'Well, does that mean he couldn't taste things either?'

'Maybe. I don't know. Why?'

Virginia shrugged.

The sound of voices drifted in from the back yard.

'Come on,' said Dorothy. She seized her sister's hand and led the way through the brightly-lit house.

Of the twenty or so mourners Vern Pierce was the only one wearing a suit. He was standing between Frank Tyler and Father Raoul, middle-aged and heavy-looking. Father Raoul, smiled as the sisters approached.

'Ladies – let me introduce Vern. Ethan's boy.'

'Pleased to meet you,' said Dorothy. She shook a stubby hand.

'Dorothy's been *so* helpful.'

'Thank you,' said Vern and he tried to smile and so did Dorothy, thinking as she did so how weird it was to be standing there talking with Ethan's son. It was only yesterday she'd found out he *had* a son, and the news, at least to start with, had unbalanced her like she'd been standing suddenly on the deck of a slow-rolling ship.

'And this,' said Father Raoul, 'is Dorothy's sister Virginia.'

Virginia stepped forward. 'Ginny, please,' she said. 'Ethan always called me Ginny.' She was smiling hard. 'Did he ever mention me?'

'Pardon me?'

'Your father. Did he ever mention me?'

Vern shook his head. The smile he'd pulled up was bleeding away. 'I don't think so,' he said.

'He probably mentioned Dorothy, though.'

Dorothy scowled at her sister.

'*They* were friends too.'

Vern nodded solemnly.

'She even stayed over sometimes. They used to go out in Ethan's car. Before they took his licence away. Didn't you, Dorothy?'

'Well –'

'They used to sit together in the movie-theater over in Wenden. Dorothy likes the movies — don't you Dorothy?'

Father Raoul cleared his throat. 'Well, if you'll excuse me, Vern, I really must circulate —'

'Me too,' said Frank.

Vern Pierce watched the two men walk away. He sipped his drink and gazed away into the gathering darkness. Suddenly he said, 'I didn't see him much.'

'Well, I expect you're busy,' said Dorothy.

'Yes,' said Vern.

Far away on the Interstate the cars were twinkling like jewels in a necklace.

Vern sipped his drink. 'In fact I didn't see him at all.' He turned to Dorothy. 'Did he tell you that?'

'Well —'

'In fact, did he tell you about me at all? Did he tell you he had grandchildren?'

Dorothy said nothing, she could feel her heart thumping.

'No?'

Grandchildren: the notion seemed absurd. 'Well maybe I forgot —'

'No,' said Vern, 'you didn't forget. Because he never told you. I suppose he never told you about Shreveport neither, or walking out on his wife like she didn't exist —'

Dorothy looked down at her hands. She felt suddenly light-headed. A wife. She'd never imagined a wife.

Vern drained his glass. 'No, I didn't think so,' he said. 'He wasn't real good at being honest.' He turned his wrist, looked at his watch. 'Anyway, I have to go.'

Dorothy looked up. 'Go? Already?'

'I said I'd be back to close up. Clare gets spooked on her own at night, I mean with just the kids —'

'Your wife?' said Dorothy.

'Uh-huh.'

'You have a business?'

'A restaurant.' Vern took out his wallet and withdrew a card. He passed it over.

VERN'S BAR AND GRILL
Vernon E. Pierce, Owner
Best Food By A Damsite!

'Clare's idea,' he said.

'She's clever.' Dorothy handed back the card.

Vern shrugged. 'Keep it if you want.'

'May I?'

'Have you ever been?'

'To Boulder City?' Dorothy shook her head.

'We've been to Las Vegas,' said Virginia.

'Oh?'

'Daddy took us. We had a big old Buick then. You know he gave us a dollar?'

'That's nice,' said Vern.

Dorothy said nothing. She was staring at the ground.

'"Don't spend it all at once," he said.'

Vern nodded.

A cool breeze swept the yard. They fell into silence.

Dorothy looked at the card, feeling it smooth in her hand. She thought of Ethan, but for a moment couldn't picture his face. It was as if suddenly – at the mention of a wife – he was lost to her. She concentrated, willing forth his image – but nothing came.

Vern looked again at his watch. 'I really must go,' he said. He looked at Dorothy, tried a smile. 'Thank you,' he said.

Dorothy shrugged, smiled back. She watched him make his way slowly through the mourners, stopping every now and then to have his hand shaken. Soon he was gone. Soon too the yard was deserted.

'Well?' said Virginia.

'Well what?'

They were standing in the kitchen, stacking glasses.

'Did you know that?'

'What?'

'About Ethan.'

Dorothy shook her head.

'Dorothy?'

16

'What?'

'I'm sorry.'

'What for?'

'For being so mean.'

'It doesn't matter.'

'It matters to me.'

Dorothy turned the taps and filled the sink. She stared at the window, at the darkness beyond. She stacked the plates with care on the drainer.

They stood beside the coffin, Ethan Pierce's last four mourners, separate in their thoughts of the dead. Frank Tyler, gazing gloomily at the coffin's gleaming handles, thought again of the town's past glories, thinking them gone for good. Dorothy meanwhile thought of Vern. She studied Ethan's face, trying to see there the face of his son, though in vain. There seemed no connection, more the absence of bonds than their presence. She studied his hands. They were pale and dry-looking, lying straight by his sides. Death, they seemed to say, is an end of everything. She swallowed hard. She glanced at Father Raoul. He smiled and took her hand in his. His flesh was warm with the warmth of life.

Virginia it was who broke the silence.

'Father?'

'Yes, Ginny?'

'I was wondering.'

'Yes?'

'Well, you know when a person dies —' She paused.

'Yes, Ginny?'

'And a person's soul is supposed to, well, fly up, to heaven or some place —'

'Yes.'

'Well, have you ever seen it?'

'Seen it?'

'A soul, I mean, flying?'

Father Raoul thought a moment, then shook his head. 'I don't believe I have, Ginny.'

'Never?'

'I don't believe so. But then I don't think it's the kind of thing a person *can* see.'

'No?'

'Well, it's a spiritual thing. Invisible to the naked eye.'

'You mean like a person's breath?'

'Yes, kind of.'

Outside, away in the distance, the dark sky rumbled.

'Father?'

'Yes, Ginny?'

'I'm sorry.'

'Sorry?'

'About this morning. Not waving to you. Will you forgive me?'

'Already did, Ginny.'

'You did?'

'Hey I knew it wasn't you, not really. It's times like these. They make people a little crazy. You just got to wait for those times to pass. Make allowances.'

'You mean, think the best of people – even when they're mean to you?'

'I suppose I do.'

Virginia looked down at Ethan Pierce, at his old man's pinched face. *You're a fool, Ginny Brinkman.* How many times had she heard him say that? She frowned. 'You mean, even when you never liked them – and they never liked you?'

'Even then, Ginny.'

She studied Ethan's mouth. It was thin and mean. Thinking good of him was too much to ask – always had been. 'I don't think I can,' she said.

'Try.'

'I've tried.'

'Well, try again.'

Sighing, she closed her eyes. At once Ethan Pierce appeared, sinking in quicksand and gasping for breath. She opened her eyes. She looked guiltily at Father Raoul.

Father Raoul was saying a prayer. His head was bowed, his hands clasped together. 'Amen,' he said finally.

'Amen,' said Dorothy.

'Amen,' said Frank.

Virginia closed her eyes again and thought again of Ethan Pierce. This time in her mind he was burning at a stake. 'Amen,' she whispered, crossing and uncrossing her fingers.

'How could you do it?'

'Do what?'

They were walking back down Constitution – Dorothy, Virginia, Frank Tyler.

'You know very well what.'

'Now come on, ladies,' said Frank. 'I hate to see you two like this. Especially now –'

'Well I'm sorry Frank, but it's *her* – acting like a fool in front of Father Raoul, saying stupid things –'

'All the same –'

'No, Frank. She's got to be told.'

'Told what?' said Virginia.

'The truth.'

'Oh, ladies –'

'No! She can't just go on ruining people's lives –'

'You're hysterical,' said Virginia. She turned coolly away. A hand on her arm turned her back.

'No you don't, missy. For once you're going to hear what I have to say.'

'Get off me! Frank, get her off me! She's hurting me! You're hurting me!'

'Right – that's it!' Frank pulled them apart, a hand on each breastbone. 'If you ladies can't be civil, then I'll thank you to be quiet.'

'But she hurt –'

'Quiet!'

They were standing on the corner by the lights. The lights flicked to green, unheeded.

'That's better now. Now, I don't want you ladies fighting no more, y'hear? I think we should all show a little respect, what with Ethan getting ready to get buried tomorrow, don't you?'

19

Dorothy looked down at her shoes. 'Yes,' she said quietly, 'you're right. I'm sorry.'

'Virginia?'

Virginia shrugged. 'I suppose.'

'Good. Then I'll be saying goodnight.'

Dorothy looked up. 'Night, Frank.' She looked tiny and frail. 'Frank?'

'Yes?'

'See you tomorrow?'

'Yes, Dorothy. Tomorrow. Sleep tight.'

'And you.'

Frank turned away and headed for home. He moved quietly through the dark empty streets. He started to whistle but gave it up. It didn't seem right. He pulled up his collar at the cool of a breeze. He was crossing his front yard when the first spots of rain began to fall.

4

PERRY JEMSON SLOWED his pick-up to a stop. The Interstate up ahead was solid — nothing to see in the darkness but brake-lights and rain. He wound down his window.

'What's going on?'

A sheriff's deputy was standing on the shoulder beside his patrol car. He was gripping his gun-belt, leaning into the rain. 'Some fucker,' he said.

'An accident?'

'Ah, some dumb fucker in a truck. Turned the fucker over.'

'Jesus,' said Perry.

'Stupid fuck.'

'Is he dead?'

The deputy shrugged. 'Fuck knows. Ain't my fucking business. That's state.'

Perry wound up his window. He switched off the engine. He looked at his watch: two fifty-two a.m. He was midway between Phoenix and Bagdad, an hour each way. He turned on the radio, but finding only talk switched it off. He picked up Philly's beat-up copy of *Weird But True Magazine* and turned the pages. Pausing at the page titled *Interesting Facts* (*About The State of Arizona*), he read:

One. Twenty-six point six per cent of the state is covered by Indian Reservations.

Two. There is a Strawberry, Arizona.

Three. The extreme northeast corner of Arizona marks the only place in the United States where four states meet. The Four Corners as they are known comprise parts of the following states: Utah, Colorado, New Mexico and Arizona.

Four. There is a Why, Arizona.

Five. Lara Lakehouse was the first woman Superior Judge in Arizona. She weighed over two hundred pounds and owned a goat called Liberace.

Six. Old gold and blue are the colors of the state.

Seven. Clifton had a jail blasted out of solid rock. The miner who did the blasting invested his paycheck in snakehead whiskey and shot up Harvey's Dance Hall. He thus became the first resident of the jail.

It was after three-thirty when the traffic started moving. Perry cruised past the ruined truck. It had been hauled onto the shoulder – you could see the marks on the road. The cab had been stove in, the windows shattered. A state trooper waved him on. Beyond the trooper a family saloon lay beaten and twisted in an arc of yellow lights. The rain beat down on it, bouncing off its carcase like marbles.

He took exit twelve and parked in the lot in back of the Dairy Queen.

'Hey, Perry.'

The restaurant was bright and empty.

'Hey, Marla.'

'What you doing out here?'

'Seeing the sights.'

Marla smiled. She was tall and had a pale angular face.

Perry ordered a banana split and a slice of blueberry pie. He took off his jacket and sat by the window. He dried his face with a handful of paper napkins.

The storm had hit the Interstate twenty miles out of Phoenix – just a light rain at first but then heavier and heavier, until the wipers had been damn near no use. There'd been thunder then, far off but getting nearer, and lightning upstate towards Flagstaff. According to the radio there were floods in Wenden and road chaos across the whole southern half of the state. The Governor – up in Utah on vacation – was said to be concerned.

Marla brought the order. She stood for a moment watching him eat.

'You wanna know something?' she said.

'What?'

She slipped into the booth and spread her hands on the table. Perry looked up from his pie. Marla was smiling.

'Look!'

He studied her hands. They were lined with years and work. A dime-store ring sat garishly on her left hand third finger.

'Congratulations,' said Perry.

She was turning it around, studying it. 'It's for eternity,' she said.

'Who's the lucky guy?'

'Oh, you wouldn't know him.'

'Out of county, then.'

'Out of state.'

Perry went back to his pie.

'What are you thinking?' said Marla.

'Nothing.'

She made her hands into fists, studying the ring. 'His name's Duane if you're interested,' she said.

'Uh-huh.'

The door to the parking lot opened. A man in a hat stood dripping at the counter, gazing up at the menu-board.

Marla pushed herself out of the booth. 'Hey, Perry,' she said. 'Don't tell no one, okay?'

'Okay,' said Perry.

He finished his pie and started on the banana split. He wasn't hungry especially, he just felt like doing something. He watched the lights of the cars on the Interstate. They were moving steadily now, west for Los Angeles, east towards Phoenix and Tucson. A shaft of lightning lit the mountains. They were rust for a moment, then lost again in the darkness and the storm.

Marla eased herself into the booth.

'So why'd you go to the City? Meet someone?'

'How'd you know I was in the City?'

'Philly told me.'

'You seen Philly?'

'Sure I did. He was in here last night. Sitting right where you're sitting. He was talking about some funeral.'

'Funeral?'

'Some old guy.'

'What old guy?'

Marla shrugged. She looked down at her hands, at the ring. 'Hey, Perry?'

'What?'

Another shrug.

'What is it?'

'Can I ask you something?'

'I guess,' said Perry.

'Well —' Marla paused, considering. 'You know when people say they love you — I mean really love you — well, how do you know if they really mean it? I mean can you tell?'

Perry shrugged. 'I guess.'

'Well, how?'

'I don't know.'

'I mean if you looked in their eyes, could you see? If you looked real hard —'

'Maybe. Why?'

Marla gazed out at the storm. Her face in the window's reflection was white, her eyes ringed with shadow.

'Marla?'

'What?'

'Ah, nothing.'

Still looking out Marla said, 'Don't say nothing. When people say nothing they mean something.'

'Well, this guy, Duane —'

Marla sat still, gazing blindly at the storm. Lightning struck the desert, suddenly illuminating the shapes of Bagdad.

'Marla —'

She sighed. 'I hate this place,' she said. Her voice was flat like a voice in a dream. 'It's a dead end. A dead dead end.'

'You could quit.'

'I can't quit. I ain't got no place else to go.'

'There's the City —'

'There ain't no City. I'm forty-nine years old. There ain't no City for me no more.'

The storm rumbled on. Rain lashed the windows.

Marla stood up. She straightened her tunic. 'I got things to do.'

She washed the floor with a mop and a bucket of water. Perry watched her for a while. He thought of the wreck on the highway and the beat-up saloon, and the lives wrecked forever by a moment's inattention. One life, one chance. One blink and it's over.

He took the backroads home, passing through Yarnell and Hillside. He stopped at Dewey for Gas. The lights in the station were out. He switched off the engine and waited. He touched the horn.

A light flickered in the window. A screen door opened.

'We're closed.'

Perry wound down the window. 'That you, Bobby?'

'Who's that?'

'Perry.'

'Well, shoot —'

'Hell, Bobby you must be getting old. You need to get yourself some glasses —'

'Oh I got glasses all right, I just ain't got the eyes —' The light flickered. 'Anyhow, what the hell you doing out here?'

'Well, Bobby, you know I was just sitting around watching TV when I said to myself why don't I go out driving and risking my life, maybe stop by old Bobby's for a beer, maybe pick up some gas —'

'Well, that's nice, Perry, real friendly, but there's a problem there —'

'What problem?'

'Well I ain't got no gas. I got beer —'

'What d'you mean you ain't got no gas? Ain't you a gas station?'

'Well I got gas all right, I just ain't got no electric. The lines are down. I can't pump the stuff.'

'But you got some put away for emergencies, right?'

'Well —'

'Ah, shit, Bobby.'

'I know, I know. I been meaning to. I just ain't got around to it.'

'You're a fool Bobby Wheeler, an old blind fool.'

'Yeah,' said Bobby. You could tell he was smiling. 'An old blind fool with Europeeen beer.'

'Carlsberg?'

'Yep. By appointment to his Highness the King of Denmark. But I don't guess you'd be interested, having to drink it with an old blind fool —'

Perry shrugged, unseen in the darkness. 'Well I guess I could stand it — long as the King of Denmark don't mind.'

'Hell, he won't mind. He's too busy ruling to mind.'

Perry splashed across the forecourt and in. The store was dark. He made his way through to the back. The back room was a storeroom that doubled as a living room, it was lit by an oil-lamp in the middle of the table. The lamp cast a yellow light, illuminating stacked boxes of cereal and soap and candy, a TV, easy chairs, a jukebox, a photograph of Ronald Reagan. In the corner a small girl was reading.

'Be right with you,' called Bobby.

The girl looked up.

'Hi, Perry.'

'Hi, Mary-Lou.'

Perry took off his jacket and hung it on the back of the door.

'What you reading?'

'Mailman Mickey. My mamma sent it. From Chicago.'

'That's nice. How is your mamma?'

Mary-Lou shrugged.

Bobby came in with a tray of beers, green and regal gold. 'Honey, it's way past time for bed. You know what time it is?'

'Aw, Daddy —'

'*Bed*. Say goodnight to Uncle Perry, now.'

Mary-Lou crossed the room and kissed Perry's cheek.

'Night, Uncle Perry.'

'Night, honey.'

'Uncle Perry?'

'Yes?'

'Are you staying over again?'

'I don't think so, honey.'

'Why not?'

'Uncle Perry's got things to do,' said Bobby. 'Now run along will you? Before Mailman Mickey sticks a stamp on your elbow and mails you to Kansas, okay?'

'Okay, Daddy.'

Mary-Lou left the room. There was the sound of light footsteps on the stairs, then overhead.

'She's cute,' said Perry.

Saying nothing, Bobby broke open the beers.

The dawn was rising when Perry left the gas station. He crossed the forecourt and sat in his truck. The storm had passed away sometime during the night, leaving behind it a day that was fresh and clear. He started the truck and pulled away. The sky was pink with the rising light, the desert vibrating with a million tiny lives. He wound down the window and leaned out. The cool desert air was jasmine-sweet.

He was a mile from Bagdad when he saw Ethan Pierce. The old man was shuffling along in the dirt by the roadside. His clothes were torn and covered with ash.

Perry drew up alongside.

'Jesus, Ethan, what the hell happened to you?'

Ethan Pierce looked up. He was unsteady on his feet and looked about to fall. His hair was wild, his face white, his eyes the eyes of a blind man.

Two

5

'I HEARD HE HAD a talk with the Lord —'

'Bullshit!'

'I beg your pardon?'

'You heard me!'

For the seventh time that morning — that calm clear morning that followed the storm — Virginia Brinkman slammed her late daddy's front door. She peered through the peephole. Charlotte Roberts (Seventh Day Baptist and, next to Ethan, the town's oldest resident) was standing on the verandah, clutching her cheek as if she'd been slapped. Virginia watched her move unsteadily down the path and into the still-wet street.

'Jesus Freak!' she called through the door.

Charlotte Roberts turned for a moment, but then hurried on.

Virginia closed the peephole. All morning they'd been coming, hoping to see Ethan — in twos and threes mostly — and all morning she'd been fending them off. Some brought flowers or small gifts while others carried nothing with which to disguise their curiosity. The news had spread fast and first to arrive was Bill Wariner, former Bell man in the county and now Editor of the *Bagdad Bugle*. He'd stood on the step, notepad shaking in his liver-spotted hand, asking ludicrous questions about Ethan's reappearance. Virginia had listened for several minutes (what use in telling him it was only that Ethan had been fooling them all or maybe Doc Peters had made a mistake in saying he was dead when he wasn't?), until the Wariner bladder had let its owner down again, forcing him to retreat in some haste. Thus far he had not returned.

A hand tapped lightly on the door. Virginia sighed and opened the peephole.

'Yes?'

Nadine Wilson, widow of Vince, long ago Manager of the Bellevue Motel, had a basket of fruit on her arm.

'Dorothy? Is that you?'

'Dorothy's asleep.'

'Oh.'

'What do you want?'

'Well, I have some fruit —'

'Okay. Just leave it.'

'Pardon?'

'On the step.'

Nadine Wilson paused.

'Yes?' said Virginia.

'Well, I was wondering —'

'Wondering what?'

'Oh nothing.' Another pause. 'It's just —'

'Just what?'

'Well I was wondering if he'd said anything —'

'Said anything? Who?'

'Ethan. If, well, he had a message for me —'

'What message?'

'From Vince. From beyond.'

Virginia closed the peephole.

'Hello?'

'You're twisted,' she said loudly.

'Pardon?'

'I said you're twisted. For God's sake, you don't think he was really dead, do you? He was just concussed or fooling or something. He hasn't been anywhere. No one's given him any messages —'

'Are you sure?'

'Oh, go away!'

Silence, then footsteps on the path.

Frank was stirring soup in the kitchen.

'Who was that?'

Virginia made a face.

He laid down the spoon.

'Ginny –'

'What?'

'You know you really must try to be more patient with people –'

'Well honestly –'

'I know, I know.'

'How can they be so stupid? How can they honestly believe that one minute he's dead and the next he gets struck by lightning that destroys the whole house and he's alive again? It's ridiculous!'

'Well –'

'Of course it is! Oh it's them old folks. One whiff of something unusual and they're standing in line to check in their minds –'

'Well they are getting on, Ginny –'

'Getting on? Getting on? I'm getting on! I'm seventy-nine years old! If I do much more getting on it'll be me that's getting messages, not him –

'All the same –'

'I know, I know. Be patient. Well I'm trying, but sometimes –'

A sound filtered down from above.

'She must be awake,' said Frank.

Virginia drew back a chair and sat down. 'He was only fooling,' she said. 'Or knocked out or something.' For a moment she laid her head in her hands, but then lifted it. 'Wasn't he, Frank?'

Frank tried the soup.

'Frank?'

'Of course,' he said. He ladled the soup into three bowls.

Dorothy was lying on her bed, her face to the wall, when Frank entered the room. He laid the tray gently on a chair.

'Dorothy?' he whispered.

She stirred but didn't wake.

He crossed the room and edged back the curtains. The sky was clear, the town quiet. At Big Bill's Autos on Main Street Perry Jemson was tinkering with a chocolate brown Toyota, the chink of his tools rising up through the warm air.

Frank left the window and sat on the edge of the bed. Dorothy was breathing steadily. He straightened the covers and waited.

The storm had gone as quickly as it had come, rolling in across the desert like a tide, then away. Thunder, silence, then the crack of lightning: Frank had listened in his bed, counting the shortening distance. Later, standing in his yard, he'd felt the trembling of the earth and the rain like stones on his face. At its height it had seemed inconceivable that the storm wouldn't change everything – that the morning when it came wouldn't be somehow different, that the town wouldn't be different, that everything wouldn't be changed forever.

He opened his eyes. Dorothy was sitting up.

'Frank?'

'Well, morning, Dorothy. How you feeling?'

She drew a hand across her brow.

'What time is it?'

'Nine, nine-thirty.'

'Where's Ginny?'

'Ginny's just fine – so don't you go worrying, okay? Here, I made you some soup.' He got up and carried the tray across the room.

'I'm not hungry.'

'Now come on, Dorothy –' He set the tray on her lap. 'You must eat –'

'Frank?'

'What?'

'Is Ethan –'

'He's next door. Sleeping.'

'In Daddy's room?'

'Have some soup, Dorothy.'

She pushed the spoon away. 'Is he really –' She frowned. 'How could it happen, Frank?'

Frank shrugged. He laid down the spoon. 'Everybody makes mistakes,' he said.

'Mistakes?'

'And Doc Peters is getting on. His eyes –'

Dorothy shook her head. 'But I saw him –'

34

'We all saw him —'

'He wasn't breathing.'

'Have some soup.'

'You saw he wasn't breathing, didn't you?'

'No, ma'am. I thought I did, but I was wrong.'

Dorothy looked down at the covers.

'He was concussed,' said Frank. 'Had to be. Otherwise —'

'Otherwise he was dead and now he's alive.'

'Exactly. And that ain't possible.'

Dorothy looked at Frank. Frank looked away.

'Well, I'll be going now,' he said.

'Frank?'

'What?'

'Nothing.'

Frank crossed the room to the door.

'Frank?'

He twisted the handle. *Otherwise he was dead and now he's alive.*

'Frank?'

Saying nothing, Frank Tyler left the room. He closed the door gently behind him.

He was walking down Main Street on his way to the store when something made him stop and turn around.

'Hey, Frankie.'

He looked up.

Philly Jemson was sitting at the curb in his pick-up.

'Heard about Ethan,' he said. He was smiling.

Frank said nothing.

Philly Jemson flicked his cigarette into the dirt. 'About how Doc Peters said the old guy was dead when he wasn't. You hear that?'

'I heard,' said Frank.

'Sure was a strange thing.'

He shrugged and walked on.

'Say, Frank?'

'What?'

'Well, I was wondering —'

Frank stopped.

'Well, suppose there'd been no storm and no lightning. Suppose he'd just gone on sleeping and sleeping until they lowered him into the ground. Wouldn't that be murder? Him being still alive and all.'

'I gotta go,' said Frank.

'Okay. See ya, Frankie.'

Frank walked on, this time away from the store.

'Hey, Frankie,' called Philly Jemson. 'Ain't you opening today?'

Saying nothing Frank walked on. There were eyes upon him. He turned on Constitution, out of their gaze.

The Pierce house was a ruin. He stood and considered it. Amongst the charred beams were the remnants of a life – the leg of a table, a chair left absurdly standing, bottles and cups, clothes and curtains burnt to ashes, the shell of a burnt-out TV.

'Crazy thing, huh?'

Reno Stuckey was standing beside him. He was holding a dark suit on a hanger.

'Well, ain't it?'

'What?' said Frank.

'Luck. I mean, take this suit.'

Reno Stuckey held up the suit. 'Moths,' he said. 'Eaten the Goddamn thing half to death.' He shrugged. 'But now it don't matter, what with there being no funeral. Say, you seen him?'

'Who?'

'Well, Ethan, of course.'

'I seen him.'

Reno Stuckey shook his head. 'Crazy thing, huh?'

'He was concussed,' said Frank.

'Yeah?'

'It was a mistake.'

Reno Stuckey whistled. 'Helluva mistake. Say, you okay?'

'I'm fine,' said Frank.

'Okay. I'll be seeing you then.'

Reno Stuckey walked away, the suit rising lazily in the breeze. Frank stared again at the remains of the house. He tried to picture it as it once had been, but could not: its absence now was stronger than memory.

He was walking away when something as before made him stop. He paused at the lights and looked up at the sky. A hawk passed over, high in the haze. Frank shielded his eyes, watching it go. It swept low to the desert, then high again, rising like a kite on the warm rising thermals. It was black against the sun, its wings quite still, its eyes like jewels in the morning.

6

'HE'S HERE,' said Virginia.

It was midday. She was standing at the window in her sister's bedroom looking down at the street.

The doorbell rang.

'Go on,' said Dorothy.

Virginia pulled a face. 'Must I?'

'Go on.'

Reluctantly she crossed the room and made her way down the stairs.

She opened the front door a crack.

'Yes?'

'It's me, Ginny.'

'Me?' Virginia yelped. 'Oh my Lord! Is it Elvis?'

Doc Peters, large and sweating, was wiping his brow with a handkerchief.

'Now come on, Ginny Brinkman, quit your fooling, alright?'

'You mean you're not Elvis?'

Doc Peters sighed. 'No, Ginny, I'm not Elvis. Now, will you let me in?'

Slowly, Virginia opened the door.

'What d'you want anyhow?'

'I've come to see Ethan.'

'I thought you said he was *dead?*'

Doc Peters stepped inside. He removed his hat. Sixty-eight years old and stooping now but still as big as a bear, his belly was vast, his hair as pale and wiry as prairie grass, his eyes – through his spectacles – watery blue.

'Now, Ginny,' he said, clasping his hat to his chest, 'I know what y'all must be thinking –'

'Oh?'

'Y'all probably thinking that old Doc Peters should be real embarrassed –'

'Yup,' said Virginia.

Doc Peters blinked twice as if he'd swallowed something sour.

'Well, Ginny, I am. And that's the truth.'

'Good.'

'I want you to know that – you and your sister –'

'Okay.'

'And also, well –' He paused. He looked down at his shoes.

'What?'

'Well, I want you to know, well, that drinking had nothing whatsoever to do with it.'

'Drinking?'

'I swear.'

Virginia shrugged. 'That's funny.'

'Pardon me?'

'I thought we were talking about *senility* not *drinking* –'

'Senility? Aw, Ginny, that ain't nice. Hell, what would your daddy say if he heard you talking to an old friend like that – specially an old friend that's trying to apologize –'

'Daddy's dead,' said Virginia.

'Well, I know that –'

She raised her shoulders, doubting. 'At least we *think* he's dead. Of course, as it was *you* as *said* he was dead he might be wandering around someplace, talking to people, having a time –'

Doc Peters looked down at his shoes.

'I mean, you never can tell, can you, Doc?'

'Aw, Ginny, be kind,' he whispered.

'Kind? Kind? You come around here, as blind as an old racoon, committing living breathing souls to the grave and you say to be kind? Well tell me, *Doctor* Peters, were you kind to poor Ethan? Aw and hell, what you blubbing for now?'

'I'm sorry,' said Doc Peters. He was dabbing at his eyes with his handkerchief. 'It's just –'

'Just what?'

'Well –'

'Well what?'

'Oh, I don't know –'

Virginia shrugged. 'Please yourself.' She turned and crossed the hall to the parlor. Doc Peters followed.

'Ginny?'

She sat down and picked up a newspaper. 'I'm busy.'

Doc Peters lowered himself onto the settee. The settee creaked.

'Look, Ginny –'

'I said I'm busy. Anyhow, shouldn't you be seeing to your patient?'

Doc Peters wiped his cheeks with his handkerchief.

'I need to talk to you Ginny – to somebody –'

Virginia looked up. 'Why?'

'Well –'

'Oh, for God's sake don't start that welling again –'

'Well, you see –'

Virginia snorted and returned to her newspaper.

'You see, I know –'

'Know what?'

Doc Peters drew a deep breath. 'Are you listening to me, Ginny?'

'Oh, I'm listening all right. You just ain't saying a whole lot.'

Doc Peters cleared his throat. He leaned forward. 'I know about Ethan,' he said.

Virginia looked up. 'You mean about the elevators?'

'Elevators?'

'Never mind.'

Doc Peters wiped his brow. 'Ginny,' he said. He licked his lips. 'Look, I know you're gonna tell me I'm crazy or something –'

'Probably.'

'Ginny, please –'

'Oh, for God's sake get on with it!'

Doc Peters bit his lip. 'Well, the thing is –'

'Yes?'

'The thing is – aw, hell Ginny, he was *dead* –'

'Who was dead?'

'Ethan!'

Virginia closed the paper. 'I know,' she said calmly.

'You *know?*'

'Frank knows too.'

'Frank?'

'He was here this morning. We were talking. He knows but he ain't saying.'

Doc Peters was shaking his head.

'So what you gonna do?' said Virginia.

'Do?'

'You gonna tell him? Somebody's got to. And Dorothy.'

Doc Peters stared down at his knees.

'Oh, Jesus,' he said.

'Drink?' said Virginia. Without waiting for an answer, she got up and crossed the room.

'Have you two been drinking?'

They were standing at the foot of Dorothy's bed. Dorothy was propped up on the pillows.

'Whiskey,' said Virginia.

'Whiskey? In the afternoon?'

'Emergency,' said Doc Peters.

'What kind of an emergency?'

He swayed slightly then corrected himself. 'Life and death,' he said gravely.

'Ethan's,' said Virginia.

Doc Peters stepped forward and sat heavily on the bed. 'Dotty,' he whispered.

His face was red. 'We've got something to tell you. A secret –' He put his finger to his lips. 'Ssh, okay?'

'You're drunk,' said Dorothy.

Doc Peters nodded. 'Had to be, Dotty.'

'Don't call me Dotty.'

He belched. 'Sorry, Dotty.'

'If this is some kind of a joke –'

Doc Peters wagged his finger. 'No joke.'

'Well, then?'

He sat himself up as straight as he was able.

'It's Ethan,' he announced.

Dorothy looked down at the covers. 'What about him?'

'He was dead,' said Virginia.

'I know.'

Doc Peters was nodding. 'For sure. I'm a doctor. Believe me.' He stopped abruptly and looked up. 'You *know*? You *too*?'

'I know,' said Dorothy. 'Frank knows too.'

'Jesus,' said Doc Peters.

Dorothy said nothing.

Doc Peters was sober now, suddenly. He licked his lips.

'Jesus, Dotty,' he said, 'what the hell are we gonna do now?'

7

NOTWITHSTANDING THE FACT that the man who'd been sitting in his bar for nigh on an hour drinking nothing but plain water and writing things down in a notebook was most probably just a salesman or a tourist or some other fool thing that he couldn't for the moment call to mind — notwithstanding this fact, just the presence of the man with his city-boy's pallor and his out-of-state accent was more than enough to make Reno Stuckey (who got nervous over which brand of candy to buy at the store) *real* nervous, not to say concerned. Or rather, suspicious. After all, whatever he was, the man was a stranger, and strangers always made Reno Stuckey suspicious.

Casual-like he moved down the bar.

'See that guy?' he whispered.

'What guy?'

'Ssh.'

Philly Jemson glanced over his shoulder. Perry was beside him, reading *Road and Track*. He looked up.

'What is it?'

'That guy,' whispered Reno.

'What guy?'

'Him.'

For the best part of an hour the man had been scribbling in his notebook, sipping his water every now and then, every now and then getting up and stepping out into the street, then coming back in and carrying on his scribbling.

'I don't like him,' said Reno.

'Then tell him to git,' said Philly.

'I can't do that. It's America we're living in, not I-ran.'

Philly shrugged.

43

Perry looked over his shoulder. 'What's he writing?'

Reno Stuckey glanced quickly at the man, then away.

'Goddamned if I know.'

'Research,' said Philly.

'Research? What do you mean research? What kind of research?'

'You mean he's a reporter?' said Perry.

'A reporter? What the hell's a reporter doing in my bar?'

Philly shrugged. He glanced at Perry, a smile already forming.

'Why don't you ask him?'

'Ask him? You mean straight out?'

'Sure.'

Reno Stuckey glanced again across the room. The man was squinting hard at his notebook, scribbling.

'Oh, I dunno. He looks kinda busy —'

'Please yourself. Hey Perry — you wanna shoot some pool?'

'I don't mind.'

'On the other hand,' said Reno, 'it *is* my bar —'

'Sure is.'

'And don't I get to say who sits and who don't sit in my bar?'

'Sure do.'

'Right.'

Reno Stuckey whipped off his apron and rounded the bar. He was red-faced and scowling when he returned.

'Sonofabitch.'

Philly was smiling. 'What's the problem, Reno?'

'You know Goddamned well what.'

'I do?'

'You sure as hell do. Guy says he's waiting for you, 'cept he don't know what you look like. Says you called him up about Ethan.' Reno Stuckey thrust his large head forward across the bar. 'How come you didn't say you knew the guy?'

Philly shrugged.

'Oh, I get it — big joke, huh? Hell, I was getting ready to punch out his lights —'

'You know him?' said Perry.

'I never met him, if that's what you mean.'

44

'But you know him?'

'Kind of.'

'Who is he?'

Philly drank the last of his beer. 'You'll see. You coming?'

8

FOR JUBAL EARLY, once of Utah's buttoned-up St George but now nominally of sprawling Los Angeles, the idea of a man being alive then dead then getting struck by lightning and coming back to life again was no more unusual – indeed a good deal less unusual – than, say (to pick other recent claims at random), a child being born with a luminous head (Emporia, Kansas), or an entire High School swimming team (Mack's Creek, Missouri) being swept up by aliens whose only means of interplanetary transport was a 1976 Oldsmobile Fairway. Indeed, so common was the whole life-after-death-after-life thing – so passé these days in the world of the strange – that had he not already been on his way down to Tombstone (where the late Hank Williams had been spotted drinking gin in a trailer-park), he'd have offered a polite but firm No Thank You, Sir and would have turned his strange mind to other things. However, as he'd be passing he'd decided to take a look, for, in the world of the off-beat, in the words of his employer Thomas J. Jackson, Owner and Editor of *Weird But True Magazine*, You Never Can Tell.

He tested his pen for ink.

'Ninety, you say?'

Perry Jemson looked at his brother. 'Isn't he?'

Philly shrugged. He was cleaning his nails with the blade of a knife. Before him on the table were two brand-new one hundred dollar bills.

'I don't know,' he said. 'He sure was old though.'

Perry turned to the bar. 'Hey, Reno. Isn't he ninety?'

'Who's that?'

'Ethan.'

Reno Stuckey paused in his polishing of a glass. His hair was

46

newly-combed, the buttons of his shirt now disguised by a tie. He rubbed his chin. 'Well, let me see now. He was ninety last birthday, so I reckon he'd be ninety-one today.'

Jubal Early squinted. His eyes were the palest blue, dark-ringed with sleeplessness. His face was thin and pale, as if he'd spent all his short life underground. 'Today is his birthday?'

'Ah, no sir. I kinda meant generally he'd be ninety-one.'

Jubal Early nodded. 'I see. I'm obliged to you.'

'Obliged?'

'For clearing that small matter up.'

Reno Stuckey looked at Philly. Philly smiled.

Subject ninety-one, wrote Jubal Early in his notebook. *Was ninety last year.*

'Can I ask you something?' said Philly.

'What?'

'Well, have you ever seen one of them poltergeists — like in the movies?'

Jubal Early was crouching over his notebook, turning the pages.

'I ain't saying I have and I ain't saying I ain't. I ain't saying nothing.' He looked up. 'Okay?'

'Okay,' said Philly. 'I was only asking.'

They sat for a moment in silence.

Jubal Early was first to speak.

'I'd be obliged,' he said, 'if I could have another glass of water.'

Reno Stuckey filled a glass from the tap and carried it over. He wiped his hands on his apron. 'You boys want a drink? On the house?'

You boys want a drink, wrote Jubal Early in his notebook. *On the house.*

Philly looked up. 'You say on the house?'

'I think he did,' said Perry.

'Sure I did. So?'

Philly smiled. 'Well, it's just you ain't said on the house since the last time your daddy asked you where the roof was.'

Reno Stuckey made a face.

Jubal Early looked up.

'I'd be obliged,' he said, 'if you'd take me to the house.'

'Now?' said Philly.

'I'd be obliged.'

Jubal Early closed his notebook and stood up. He was taller than he'd seemed he'd be sitting down, and leaner. His dark suit was frayed at the cuffs and lapels. His shoes were brown and dusty.

'One thing,' he said. He paused.

'What?'

Jubal Early narrowed his eyes. He looked from one brother to the other and back. 'I ain't saying I believe yous, all right?' He shook his head. 'No sir. I ain't saying that.'

'Sure thing,' said Philly. 'Whatever you say.'

'I ain't one of them believing fools – right?'

'Right.'

'Right.'

Jubal Early put on his hat. It was an old-time preacher's hat, black with a wide brim. 'Just as long as you and me's clear on that one point.' He glanced at Perry. Perry was staring at the ground, teeth clenched, trying not to laugh.

'Man, he's weird, ain't he? You sure he ain't escaped from someplace?'

'California,' said Philly, shielding his eyes from the sun. 'What the hell's he doing now?'

Jubal Early was down on his haunches talking to an old man in a station-wagon. The old man was shaking his head.

'Isn't that Lester Snipe?'

Perry shrugged.

Down the street, Jubal Early was peeling off a note from his money-roll. He passed it through the station-wagon's window.

'It *is* Lester Snipe,' said Philly. 'That sonofabitch.'

'What's the problem?'

'The problem is, little brother, that that Goddamn Lester Snipe just stole some of our money.'

'What do you mean our money?'

'Jesus, Perry, will you wake up? The guy's weird – right?'

'Yeah – so?'

'So he's also loaded. You see that roll? Well that's our roll. It ain't meant for no asshole like Lester Snipe.'

'Well, we can't stop him,' said Perry.

'Sure we can.'

'Yeah – how?'

From his pocket Philly pulled out a knife. The blade flicked up.

'Jesus, Philly. You're a fucking maniac.'

Philly moved close, nose to nose. 'Oh yeah?'

Perry turned away. From out of nowhere Jubal Early was standing behind him on the curb. He raised his preacher's hat.

'Nice fella,' he said. 'Obliging.'

Philly turned, scowling. 'What the hell you doing there?'

'I heard voices. Thought you might need a preacher.'

'You ain't no preacher.'

'No, sir. But I have heard confessions.'

'What?'

'In my time.'

'Look,' said Philly, he was scowling harder.

'Leave it,' said Perry.

Jubal Early withdrew the money-roll from the folds of his coat. He peeled off four hundreds.

'I believe it's the Brinkman house,' he said. 'Leastways, that's what I've been informed.'

Philly took the money. He scowled at Perry.

'You show him. I got things to do.'

Philly stalked away, across the street, through an abandoned yard. Perry watched him go.

Jubal Early was adjusting his hat.

'Shall we go, sir?' he said.

'Okay,' said Perry, looking out one last time for his brother. There was no sign now, just silence. He turned away. 'This way,' he said.

The sun was high in the sky as they turned on Constitution, the sky arching blue above the shadowless town.

'You live in Los Angeles?' said Perry. They were walking past the old Nichols' place.

49

'Pardon me?,' said Jubal Early.

'Los Angeles. Is that where you live?'

'No, sir.'

'No? Where then?'

'Los Angeles, but I ain't living there. It ain't no place for a person to live.'

'Ain't it?'

Jubal Early shook his head. 'I just keep my things there. The rest of the time I'm moving around. Scotland, Canada, Ivory Coast.'

Perry whistled. 'Jesus – you been to those places?'

'Zambia, Gambia, Fiji, Fuji, Uptown, Downtown, Hip-Hop, Don't Stop, Chittagong, Sing-A-Song. Sure I have.'

Perry said nothing. They walked on. In a while he sneaked a look. Jubal Early was staring straight ahead as he walked, his hat pulled low, no trace of a smile. His face was smooth like a child's, but there was something about it that made you feel there'd be lines on the inside. He paused beside a tree and removed his hat.

'Sure is hot,' he said.

'Sure is,' said Perry.

From the folds of his coat, Jubal Early withdrew the money-roll. He peeled off six hundreds.

'I'm obliged to you.'

'For what?'

'Your assistance.'

Perry took the money. 'Don't you want me to show you the house?'

'I believe I can find it.'

Perry shrugged. 'It's a ways off –'

Jubal Early resettled his hat. 'I'm obliged,' he said, and walked on.

9

THAT DAY, the day that followed Ethan Pierce's reappearance, Frank Tyler didn't open the store. Instead, coming back from the Pierce house, he sat in his yard drinking beer and staring out at the desert, trying to make sense of what he'd seen. But sense wouldn't come. What he'd seen didn't make any sense. A man doesn't die then come back – doesn't lie cold and lifeless in his coffin, only, come a storm, to revive. Death is irreversible: he knew that.

But still –

He drew a hand across his brow. It was past midday now, the sun high in the sky, but still he couldn't winkle out the sense in things, couldn't dismiss the wildest of his thoughts. He looked down at his dusty shoes. Sometimes there seemed no sense in anything any more.

It was cool in the house. He lay down on his bed and closed his eyes. Shapes pitched and swirled, then settled. *What can you see?*, said his father in a sudden dream, close up. Soon, in the eye of his mind, he was standing in a dark room, looking down upon his father's pale face. His father's eyes were open but blind, his cheeks sunk deep in shadow and coarse to the touch of lips.

What can you see?

Nothing, father.

He turned on his bed in his beery sleep, a boy again taking his leave.

His father's passing when it came came silently, a life sneaked away like a wallet lifted stealthily from a pocket. No final grasp of hands or meaningful looks or advice to pass on. Just silence suddenly, an absence of breathing, an unremarkable ceasing. He'd stood for a while that day, staring, expecting something more, until his mother had led him away. The following week they'd stood at a graveside holding hands.

He woke abruptly. The sun was burning behind the blind. He sat up. His head was throbbing from the beer. He edged up the blind. Far off, needle-thin and silver in the lap of the vast ochre mountains, the Desert Express was crossing the state, heading for Phoenix and all points east. He watched it go until it was gone. He lowered the blind.

10

'WELL?'

'Well what?'

'Well, aren't you going to do something?'

'Me?'

'Yes, you.'

Doc Peters looked down at the body in the bed. The old man's face was white, his hair a tangle, his breath coming regular but shallow. 'But what if he wakes up?'

'I thought that was the idea,' said Virginia.

'Go on,' said Dorothy.

They were standing — the three of them — around the late Judge Brinkman's broad and bowed four-poster. The room was gloomy, the curtains closed, the air thick with breathing.

Doc Peters swallowed hard. He looked from one sister to the other. There was no escape. 'Aw, shoot,' he said. He approached the bed. He'd had a feeling all day something bad was going to happen.

11

JUBAL EARLY HEARD the shriek — a woman's — coming from the upstairs bedroom. He was standing in the shadows of an abandoned yard across the street from the Brinkman house. He raised his hat and cocked an ear. For an hour he'd been waiting for something to happen, and now it had. Replacing his hat, he withdrew his notebook from the folds of his coat. He rested the notebook on a low stone wall. He unclipped a pen from his inside pocket. *The natives are restless*, he wrote carefully.

Three

12

TODAY, SHOULD YOU find yourself poolside at the Bagdad Best Western (formerly the Bellevue Motel), and should the events of that summer still be fresh in your mind, then let your eye wander west along Main to Constitution, then north three blocks to the old Brinkman place. Preserved forever (or as long as interest holds) by the authorities of Ethan Pierce County (formerly Bill Williams County), the house, today, is just as it was then all those years ago, except in one respect. These days, when the last visitor from Tokyo or Tulsa or some other exotic place has gone and the doors have been locked for the night, those rooms where the sisters and Frank and Doc Peters once trod and where Ethan Pierce was shaken awake from his dream of death are quiet now, rooms full of shadows and stillness, as cool in the darkness as the blue cooling desert. No voices echo now through the hall and no footsteps fall on the stairs, and only in the minds of the curious does the scene now replay: Doc Peters, huge and sweating, and the sisters – one tall and slight, the other shorter, darker – standing together in their father's gloomy room, looking down at the low-breathing body in the bed. Only in the minds of these passing tourists does that which once happened there happen once again. They pause on the landing and peer into the room, at the dipping four-poster and the frames filled with faces on the dresser, and there – in their minds' eyes – does Ethan Pierce wake as he woke on that day. His hair stands up as it stood up then, and his eyes twinkle brightly with lewd intention. He leers again as he leered on that day and in the movie and, as they did on that day, his hands snake their way up a lady's pleated skirt. Dorothy shrieks and Doc Peters faints, and all once again for a moment is chaos. But then the moment passes and the visitors move on. They stand in the front yard and load their cameras; they wait for their buses and lick ice-creams. Some cross the road to the souvenir booth and sit on a low stone wall. They get up, chattering; a bus pulls away. In time the night rolls in and over like a fog. Silence rises. Dust falls.

13

'IT'S DISGUSTING!'

'Revolting!'

'I mean – a man of his age!'

Nobody knew, in the days that followed, what had happened in that room at the Brinkman house, though everyone was sure that what had happened was foul. Of the three who'd been there, two were unavailable and the third wasn't saying. Doc Peters, on coming to from his faint, had fled for his life to his sister's place in Kansas, and Dorothy – the victim – had taken to her bed. And Virginia? Well, questions had been asked of her, but all – like now – had been coolly rebuffed.

'Wouldn't you say so, Ginny?'

Virginia shrugged. 'I don't know what you're talking about,' she said.

'Oh come on, Ginny!'

Fixing her face (giving nothing away), Virginia replaced the bag of oranges on the shelf in the store.

Rona Marabar touched her arm, smiling understandingly, revealing as she did so her snow-white false teeth.

'Look, dear,' she whispered, 'we're all friends here. You can tell us.'

Virginia pulled away.

Rona Marabar dropped the smile. She bristled. Her friends bristled too.

Frank Tyler looked out from the storeroom.

'Ladies? Is everything all right?'

Rona Marabar, her head in the air, led her friends in silent protest from the store. The store for the moment was quiet.

'Ginny? Are you okay?'

Virginia was staring at the shelves. She shrugged and suddenly there were tears. 'Oh, Frank,' she said. She covered her eyes. 'What's happening?'

Frank crossed the room and held her tight. She was tiny in his arms.

'Frank?'

'Ssh.'

'Oh, Frank.'

'It's all right.'

Virginia looked up. Her face was pale. 'What are we going to do?'

Frank said nothing.

'Frank?'

'I don't know.'

'We've got to do something.'

'What?'

'We could tell him to leave. You could tell him. He'd listen to you.'

'Me?'

'You were his friend.'

Frank looked out at the street.

'Please,' said Virginia.

The street looked hard in the harsh noon light.

'Frank? Will you do it? Will you talk to him?'

'Okay,' said Frank.

'Now?'

He sighed. 'Alright,' he said.

14

THOSE DAYS, in the days before McDonald's invaded the town, before Denny's and Burger King, before the Bagdad Best Western and the fleets of summer cars – before all this, before the town's advancement – you could stand on the corner of Main and Constitution and see just about all there was to see. Big Bill's Autos, the Bagdad General Store, the sidewalks and houses fading into the dust – all then was visible with one sweep of the eye, all laid bare at a glance.

'What are you doing?'

'Pardon me?'

Rona Marabar, bristling still from Virginia's brusque manner in the store, drew her ladies to a stop on the corner. She looked with disdain at the stranger.

'Are you lost?'

Jubal Early shook his head. His pallor was extreme (especially so when contrasted with the blackness of his hat); it was a pallor, he knew, disconcerting to women. 'I'd be obliged,' he said.

'Obliged?'

He loomed suddenly forward, sharp like a spindly crow, startling Rona Marabar who stepped back.

'I'd be obliged if you ladies would step aside.'

'What?'

'Step aside.'

'Why?'

Jubal Early frowned. He knew there is information to be gained from a town by uninterrupted looking, though he didn't say so. Instead he said nothing.

'Come,' said Rona Marabar. 'The man's obviously an imbecile.' She turned pointedly away, the ladies following.

Jubal Early watched them go. He pulled out his notebook from his pocket. He unclipped his pen. *Midday*, he wrote in his long sloping hand, then, writing nothing further, he replaced the notebook and settled his hat. He glanced again at his watch.

For two days Jubal Early had not been idle. In the name of research, he'd crept unseen through the yards of the town, peering over window-sills and eavesdropping casual talk. Under cover of night he'd climbed a tree in the Brinkman yard, sitting quiet amongst the branches, watching, listening. In the dawn's eerie stillness he'd eased across the yard and turned his thief's keys in the lock. He'd gazed in the moonlight upon the face of Ethan Pierce. He'd listened with interest to the man's beating heart.

He was crossing the forecourt of Big Bill's Autos when the sense of eyes upon him made him stop.

He narrowed his eyes.

A yellow 73 Toyota was sitting unattended in the workshop. A radio was playing.

He checked the office and the men's room. He stood in the doorway. 'I can see you,' he lied.

He turned at a sound.

Philly Jemson was down on his haunches in the corner. He'd been watching all the time.

The watcher watched, thought Jubal Early.

'Interested?'

Jubal Early frowned.

'The Toyota. She's worth fifteen.'

Jubal Early shook his head.

'No?'

'I ain't driving.'

Philly Jemson straightened up against the wall.

'Sure you are. Everybody's driving.'

'No, sir.'

'No, sir?'

Philly Jemson was smiling. His overalls were streaked with

dirt. From the corner of his eye, Jubal Early could see he had grease-dirt hands, as dark as a negro's.

'Everybody's driving,' said Philly Jemson.

'Well, I ain't.'

Philly Jemson flicked a rivet across the workshop. It clattered in a corner. 'You seen the old man yet?' He was smiling still. His face was tanned and hard.

Jubal Early said nothing.

'Well?'

'Well, I ain't saying.'

'So you have.'

'I said I ain't saying.'

'Okay.'

Jubal Early turned away.

'Hey, Jubal.'

'What?'

'What kind of a name is that? Jubal?'

'It's a name.'

'I know it's a name.'

Jubal Early took a step towards the street.

'Hey, Jubal —'

He stopped.

'You seen my brother?'

He shook his head.

'You sure now?'

'I ain't seen your brother.'

'Well, I bet you have.'

Jubal Early shrugged. There was something in Philly's voice that was suddenly different: the menace in the voice had eased; it was suddenly more the voice of a boy. 'I said I ain't seen him,' he said.

Philly Jemson flicked another rivet. 'Well, if you do,' he said, 'will you tell him to come on home?'

Jubal Early said okay and walked on. There were eyes upon him as he crossed the street.

He was standing in the shadows by the side of the museum

when he saw Perry Jemson go by. Perry Jemson was at the wheel of a pick-up, his eyes set straight ahead. He looked nervous. The pick-up paused a moment at the lights. The lights changed.

15

IT WAS A little after two when Father Raoul pulled up at the curb across the road from the Brinkman house and switched off his engine. He sat for a moment gazing at the dials on his dashboard and thinking. He thought about Virginia and especially Dorothy and how best he might help them to cope with Ethan's loss. He would, he decided, take the life-must-go-on route, not only because it seemed appropriate but also because he believed it. Life does have to go on, if life is to have any meaning.

He checked his look in the mirror and sat a moment longer, gathering his thoughts. In a yard somewhere a dog was barking. A voice rose up, sharp, accusing. The barking stopped.

He was peering through the front door's glass panel (there was no reply to his knocking) when he sensed someone watching him, behind him. He turned.

Jubal Early was standing at the end of the path. He raised his hand.

'I'm obliged,' he said.

'Excuse me?' said Father Raoul.

'That is to say I would be obliged.' Jubal Early paused. 'That is to say if you don't mind —'

'Mind what?'

From the folds of his coat Jubal Early produced a tiny camera. This he held up to his eye, closing the other in a squint. The shutter clicked. He lowered the camera.

'Who are you?' said Father Raoul. 'What do you want?'

'I'm obliged,' said Jubal Early, raising his hat again and smiling palely. He turned and walked away. In a moment he was gone from sight.

Father Raoul stood for a minute gazing out across the street. Then a truck rattled by raising dust from its wheels. He made his way slowly around the side of the house.

He was cupping his hands to the kitchen window, peering in, when he heard voices — Frank and Virginia — in the front yard. He made his way back around the house.

The front door was open. He stepped inside. The hall was cool and silent.

'Hello?' he called.

He tried the lounge. Nothing. He climbed the stairs.

Virginia was standing in an open doorway. She turned when she heard him. Frank Tyler turned too.

Father Raoul touched the bannister. 'Ginny? Are you all right? Frank?'

'He's gone,' said Virginia.

'Gone? Who's gone?'

Frank stepped back, he looked unsteady. 'Ethan,' he said. 'Through the window.' He looked at Virginia. Her face, like his, was pale.

WHEN JUBAL EARLY returned to the garage he found it deserted, the radio off. He checked around just to make sure and when he was sure he eased himself in behind the wheel of the yellow Toyota. He tested the pedals and reset the mirror as he'd seen people do. He braced himself and twisted the key. Heavens, he thought, as the engine rumbled loud. He eased off the handbrake. His heart was thumping.

PERRY FOUND A booth in the corner of the Dairy Queen and slid in. He studied the menu. In a while Marla sat down beside him.

'You okay?'

Perry shrugged.

Marla splayed her fingers on the table. 'See?' she said.

'See what?'

Her nails were bitten, the dime-store ring she'd been so proud of gone. She curled her fingers into fists. 'I told him,' she said.

'What?'

'Duane. I told him to quit lying and leave me be. I looked in his eyes like you said. He was lying for sure.'

Perry said nothing.

'Course he denied it — he was pleading and crying — but then a liar would, wouldn't he?'

'I guess,' said Perry.

A voice called out from the counter.

'All right!' said Marla. She pushed herself out of the booth. She touched Perry's arm. She looked suddenly grave. 'I ain't sorry I did it,' she said.

Perry smiled. The voice called again from the counter.

'Okay!'

Marla's hand lingered a moment longer. 'You eating?' she said. Her hand was warm.

Perry ordered a Coke and a piece of blueberry pie.

Marla smiled like a little girl and turned away. Her hair at the back was out of its clips.

Perry gazed out of the window. In the parking lot a man in a crumpled suit was sorting through boxes in the trunk of his car. Beyond him, a thin woman in a baseball cap was scolding a child, jabbing her finger, pointing at the girl's dusty shoes. The woman's voice rose up, sharp but unintelligible through the glass. Perry watched them for a while. Then a rig passed by heading for the highway, east or west, horn blaring, metal gleaming, and mother and child were gone from sight.

'So where're you going?'

Marla set down the pie and Coke. Her lips were freshly rouged.

Perry shrugged. He thought of Philly. By now Philly would be wondering where he was. He pushed the thought away.

'Phoenix?' said Marla.

'Maybe.'

'Don't you know?'

'I said maybe.'

Marla shrugged. 'Please yourself.' She turned away. Later, when three o'clock came, she was nowhere to be seen. Perry left two dollars on the table and went out to the truck. He knew he would never see Marla again.

He didn't look back as he crossed the county line. He knew if he did that the ties of blood that bound him to the South and to his brother would slow him and draw him back. Instead, he looked straight ahead as he drove, out across the desert to the shimmering highway, towards Aquila and Wenden, towards the blue restless mountains, towards the rest of America and the rest of his life. He tuned the radio to a country station. *Blow*, sang a voice, *Seminole Wind, blow like you're never gonna blow again*. He touched the gas. The pick-up sped on.

18

FROM THE WINDOW of her room above the Dewey gas station, Mary-Lou Wheeler watched the figure approaching. She'd been watching, her chin in her hands, ever since the speck had appeared on the distant horizon. Now, still perhaps a quarter-mile away, the figure stopped. He dropped to his haunches and re-tied his laces. Mary-Lou shifted on her chair. The man – an old man, she could see now – straightened up and continued his walking. Soon, through the warm still air she could hear singing:

> *'I'M a Yankee doodle DANdy,*
> *YANKee doodle do or DIE!'*

She pressed her nose to the glass. Despite the old man's pure white hair that made him look a hundred, he'd a young man's jaunty walk, and his eyes – though pale with age – held within them the bright light of youth. Gradually, step by carefree step, he advanced. As he passed beyond the pumps, shirt-tails flapping, he raised his hands high above his head and started scything the air as if he were conducting an invisible band. He marched out past the dry well and the empty shed that had once been the tire shop, disappearing for a while then coming back into view a mile on. Mary-Lou watched him move like a beetle down the road. In time he tipped over the horizon and was gone. She stared at the heat-haze a moment then raced down the stairs to tell her father.

Bobby Wheeler was out back, drinking in the shade of the old lean-to.

'What is it, honey?' he said. He was squinting in the harsh light. His hair was a mess.

Mary-Lou stared hard at the bottle. She shrugged.

'Honey?'

'Nothing,' she said.

Bobby looked down at his boots, muscles flexing in his cheeks.

'Daddy?'

'What?'

'You promised.'

He looked up. 'I didn't promise you.'

'You promised mama.'

'Well mama ain't here.'

'But she will be.'

Bobby shrugged.

'Won't she?'

'I don't know,' he said.

'But you said –'

'I said I don't know, alright?'

Bobby raised the bottle to his lips, closing his eyes as he drank. Mary-Lou stood in silence, watching. She thought of the old man with the white hair and wondered if he was a drunk too.

Bobby lowered the bottle. He wiped his face on his sleeve. He looked up. 'What is it?'

Mary-Lou shrugged. 'I saw a man,' she said.

'What man?'

'An old man. With white hair. He was singing.'

'Singing?'

'And waving his arms.'

Bobby shook his head. He looked down at his dusty boots.

'Daddy?'

'Look, Mary-Lou –'

'What?'

'Ah, nothing.'

'Daddy?'

'What?'

'How far's Chicago?'

Bobby shrugged.

'Is it a long way?'

'I guess.'

'What's it like?'

Bobby Wheeler, who'd never been to Chicago (in fact he'd

never been further than Denver), looked out across the desert to the mountains as if he thought he might find it there. He took off his cap and wiped the sweat from his forehead.

'Daddy?'

He replaced the cap, pulling it down. 'Well, it ain't Dewey,' he said.

BACK THEN, there was a deal of debating in the county over whether Lennie-May Wheeler had left her husband and gone to Chicago to live with her sister Sherene because her husband was a drunk, or whether her husband was a drunk because his wife had left him and gone to Chicago, leaving him in the process with a run-down gas station and debts he couldn't pay, not to mention a seven-year-old daughter who should be in school and wasn't. Which it was, nobody knew for sure. Except Perry Jemson. He knew. He knew because he'd known Lennie-May. He knew better than anyone that Lennie-May Wheeler could turn the good Lord Himself to drink.

Now, with Lennie-May long gone, Perry slowed at the gas station and looked up at the upstairs front window. The window was empty now, unattended, the room within quiet and still like a picture in a frame. He touched the gas and cruised past the old tire shop. He glanced in his mirror. *You know you're the one, Perry.* For a moment Lennie-May was standing again in the shadows, smoking a cigarette and beckoning. Perry turned his eyes away. He looked back; of course she was gone. He gripped the wheel and drove on.

He was five miles from Wenden when for the second time in three days he passed Ethan Pierce by the roadside. He stopped the truck and backed up. He wound down the window.

Ethan Pierce was smiling broadly. 'Hi, kid.' His hair was wild like Albert Einstein's, his pale eyes as bright as a child's. He was wearing Judge Brinkman's old dinner-suit, which was several sizes too big, and large polished oversized shoes. 'Where you headed?' he said.

'What?'

'I'm headed for Flag. You headed for Flag?'

Perry shook his head. 'Jesus, Ethan, how the hell did you get out here?'

Ethan held up his thumb. He dropped the smile. 'You alright, kid? You look kinda pale. Hey, you think I should drive?'

'What?'

'If you ain't feeling too good, I mean.'

Perry sighed.

'This one of them automatics?'

'What?'

Ethan was peering inside the cab. 'Now you know I ain't handled a ve-hicle for some time, but I reckon when you know how you know how for good.' He gripped the doorhandle. 'Whaddayasay, kid? You gonna let the old fella drive?'

Perry closed his eyes. Last he'd heard there'd been some mix-up, Doc Peters calling the old boy dead when he wasn't, when all the time he was just sick. 'Look,' he said, 'I don't know what the hell you're doing out here —'

'Walking, kid, just walking —'

'Walking?'

''Cept maybe I'm driving now.' Ethan smiled. 'Whaddayasay? You gonna let me drive?'

Perry shook his head. This he didn't need. 'You can't drive. You ain't got no license no more. And besides —' He studied the old man's face. 'Ain't you supposed to be sick or something?'

Ethan stuck out his tongue. It was pink and healthy. 'Oh, I ain't sick,' he said. ''Cept maybe of them.' He nodded over his shoulder, back the way he'd come. 'Goddamn fussing all the time, feeding me Goddamn soup —'

The pick-up's engine coughed and stalled.

'*Jesus*,' said Perry. This he didn't need either.

'Trouble, kid?'

'Oh, for God's sake stop calling me kid, will you?'

'Okay. You want me to take a look?'

'You?'

'Sure. Why not?'

'You a mechanic now?'

'Well not exactly –'

'Exactly,' said Perry. He circled the truck and opened the hood. He bent low over the engine. Standing behind him, Ethan peered over his shoulder.

'It's your battery, kid.'

'I know,' said Perry.

'She ain't holding a charge.'

Perry yanked off the distributor cap. 'I said I know, didn't I?'

Ethan whistled. 'She sure is filthy –'

Perry turned fast, banging his head on the hood.

'Hey, kid –'

'Don't call me kid!'

'Who's that?'

'What?'

'That!'

Perry peered around the edge of the hood.

The truck's cover was back, a figure emerging.

'Well, hello,' said Ethan.

'Hi there,' said Marla. She beamed at Perry. 'Surprise!'

20

MARY-LOU WHEELER was dropping stones down the well when she saw the yellow car approaching. The car was traveling fast, raising a plume of dust, weaving and shimmering in the heat off the road. She stood a while watching. When she heard the engine — a tiny clattering sound — she ran across the yard and into the office.

Bobby Wheeler was asleep and snoring in the back room. She shook his arm. He stirred but didn't wake.

'There's a car coming, Daddy,' she said.

The car grew louder.

'Daddy?'

It screeched to a stop. A door opened.

'Daddy?'

Mary-Lou tugged on her father's sleeve, but still he wouldn't wake. She peered through the doorway to the office and beyond. A tall spindly man in a hat was standing by his car looking up and down the road as if he was lost or expecting something. He squinted at the office, shielding his eyes.

Mary-Lou gave up on her father and crossed the yard. She stopped at the well.

'I can't give you no gas,' she said.

The stranger raised his hat. His face was pale, his clothes worn and dusty. 'Well, I ain't looking for no gas,' he said.

'What you want then? We ain't got tires no more.'

'I ain't looking for no tires neither. I'm looking for a man, drives a white pick-up. You seen such a vehicle driving by?'

Mary-Lou shook her head.

'You been looking?'

'Sure I been looking.'

'All the time? You ain't looked away for a tiny moment or closed your eyes?'

Mary-Lou shrugged. The man was spooky, like a ghost.

'And you ain't seen such a vehicle?'

'I told you. I ain't seen no pick-up.'

'You sure now?'

Mary-Lou said nothing. She watched the man get back into the car. He wound down the window.

'Anyway,' he said, 'I'm obliged.' He ground the gear-shift and the car lurched away. It weaved across the road, disappearing in a cloud of dust.

21

PERRY JEMSON HAD planned by now to be half way to Albuquerque, maybe sitting in a bar someplace contemplating the
road to come, and he would have been if fate hadn't stepped in
in the shape of a low-charging battery, leaving him stuck by the
roadside with a sullen-faced Marla and old Ethan Pierce gone
crazy.

He looked from one to the other.

'Whaddaya mean you're coming too? You can't come too.'

'Why not?' said Marla.

'Well, in the first place you don't know where I'm going, and
in the second place wherever it is I'm going I'm going on my
own, alright?'

Ethan shook his head.

'Why're you shaking your head?'

'Well in the first place, kid, you ain't going no place.' He
rapped his knuckles on the battery.

'Ah, Jesus,' said Perry. For a moment he'd forgotten.

'Perry?' said Marla.

'What?'

'I thought you'd be glad.'

'Glad? About what?'

She looked down at her new but now dusty shoes. 'I thought
you wanted me to come.'

Perry closed his eyes for a moment. He sighed.

'I told Duane about you and everything. That's why we broke
up.'

'Look, kid,' said Ethan.

'Don't call me kid!'

'Sorry, kid.'

And then Marla was crying and Perry was thinking any minute I'll wake up. He looked at Ethan. Ethan was smiling.

'What the hell're you smiling about?'

Ethan shrugged. 'Seems to me, kid, you got yourself a problem.'

Unseen, a yellow car was moving fast towards them on the road. It was weaving this way and that, raising a column of dust.

'Look,' said Perry, trying to sound calm, which he didn't feel, 'don't you understand? I can't take passengers. Marla? Do you understand? Marla? Are you okay?'

Marla was staring over his shoulder at the road.

'Look!'

'What?'

'Jesus Christ,' said Ethan.

And then suddenly the car was upon them, motor raving, tires spitting stones. It swerved, raising dust-clouds, its back end spinning and clipping the pick-up, sending the pick-up's hood crashing down. Then, just as suddenly, it was clattering away, racing up the road like a scalded cat, the rattle of its engine growing feinter with every mile until it dipped over the horizon and was gone.

Ethan picked himself up. He was covered with dust. 'Jesus Christ, kid, who the hell was that?' He looked about him. 'Kid?' Marla was crouching beside the pick-up, her hands covering her face. 'Where are you, kid?'

Perry was lying on the road beyond the pick-up. There was blood on his temple. He opened his eyes at the stinging touch of hands.

'Kid? Are you all right?'

He opened his mouth. His mouth was dusty, full of dirt.

A hand slapped his face.

'Speak to me, kid!'

The light was glarey and then he was floating and then he was tumbling and then there was blackness, then nothing.

22

JIMMY CHAI DROVE the long way home that day, along the desert tracks he'd often walked as a boy. He held the wheel loosely, spinning it through his hands as the pick-up's springs stretched then bunched on the uneven ground, jolting his bones and rattling the jewelry boxed up in the back. He leaned over and turned up the radio. The signal was poor: interference from the testing station at Las Viejas. He switched the radio off, listening instead to the engine and the whispering sound of his wheels on the sand.

He slowed at the railroad and paused. The line was empty either way, rails rippling in the heat. He crossed the tracks and drove on.

Sometimes on his way home Jimmy Chai imagined he was driving not to the Pueblo but away from it, towards another, different life. This life he imagined was always the same other life: a life lived off of the Reservation, a life without jewelry, without silver pendants and malachite earrings, a life that meant not standing all day behind a table in a rest area, a life without tourists, without the dust that clogs your eyes, without the cars spitting stones out on Interstate Ten. Some days this new life seemed so close he could almost touch it; other days like today it just seemed ridiculous — about as likely to happen as he was to make President.

He tried the radio again. Still no good. He flicked it off. He stared ahead, thinking nothing.

At first when he saw the pick-up away on the road he thought it was tourists stopping for the view, but when he got nearer he could see there was trouble. There was an old man and a girl. They were kneeling beside someone else who was lying flat on the road. Jimmy turned the pick-up towards them. He bumped across the scrub and up onto the road. He pulled up alongside.

'What happened?'

'He got hit,' said the girl.

'Is he dead?'

The old man looked up. His face was white like he'd seen a ghost. 'Kid needs a doctor,' he said.

Jimmy looked down at the body.

'Is he breathing?'

The boy's shirt was ripped. There was blood on his cheek. There were marks on the road where he'd been dragged.

'Did you see who did it?'

The old man shrugged. He touched the boy's forehead. The boy stirred, opening his eyes.

'Ethan?'

'Kid!'

'What happened?'

The girl leaned forward. Her face was streaked with dirt and tears. 'Oh, Perry, we thought you were dead! Perry?'

'He passed out,' said Ethan. 'We got to get him to a doctor.' He looked up. 'You know a doctor?'

Jimmy squinted up the road.

'Gallup?'

'What?'

'Maybe Holbrook?'

'Ain't there nobody nearer?'

Jimmy shrugged.

'Ain't you people got doctors?'

'What do you mean?' said Jimmy. '*You people?*'

'He means on the Reservation,' said Marla. She glared at Ethan, then looked up trying to smile. 'Ain't you got nobody?'

Jimmy shrugged. 'There's Agnes, yeah.' He looked at Ethan who was looking down at the boy. 'But she ain't one of *you.*'

'He don't mean nothing,' said Marla. 'He's upset, is all.'

'Sure,' said Jimmy. He looked at Marla. 'You and your boy-friend wanna sit in the cab?'

'What about Ethan?'

Jimmy started the pick-up. He gunned the engine. 'Grandad's in the back,' he said. 'With the scalps.'

23

SANTO DORINGO PUEBLO sat squatting like a bunch of hogs in the sun, round-shouldered and hunched, the color of the land.

Jimmy parked the family pick-up outside the store. 'Wait here,' he said. He disappeared inside. When he emerged it was with a woman, thirtyish, in a bright print dress. The woman was dark-skinned with blue-black hair drawn back from her face and secured with a bow. She was carrying a bag. She talked with Jimmy a moment, then walked briskly to the first of the low adobe houses.

They laid Perry Jemson on a bed in a dark low-ceilinged room. The air in the room was cooled by a rattling fan.

'Will he be okay?' said Marla.

The woman in the print dress was listening to Perry's chest. She held up her hand for silence. In a while she sat up. 'Are you family?' she said.

Marla felt a dagger spear her heart.

'Is he —'

The woman smiled. She had a clear kind face. 'He'll be fine,' she said. 'He needs rest.'

'Are you sure?' said Ethan.

'Positive.'

The woman stood up. She picked up her bag. 'Are you his sister?'

'I'm his girlfriend,' said Marla.

'Then you won't mind sitting with him?'

Marla held Perry's hand as the others left the room. She touched his forehead. It was hot. Perry stirred, saying something in his sleep she didn't catch. 'Ssh,' she whispered, then she heard a thumping close at hand. She held her breath, listening, and then it came to her what it was. It was the sound of her own heart beating.

24

LIEUTENANT TOM KATON of the Navajo Tribal Police was round-ing Blue Mesa when he got the hit-and-run call. He slowed his patrol car and turned it around. He felt lousy. He touched the gas and headed east towards the Pueblo. He could hear his gut grumbling.

All morning since the breakfast he'd missed again (fixing breakfast for one always seemed too much trouble and too lonesome a thing to do) he'd been trying to take his mind off his hunger by trying to remember (if remember was right as maybe he'd never known it) the capital of Peru. Now, as he left the highway and started down the dirt road to the Pueblo it came to him. He touched the button on his radio.

'Yes, Lieutenant?'

'Caracas,' he said.

'No, sir.'

'What?'

'That's Venezuela, sir.'

He banged the wheel with his palm. He could just imagine John Henio smiling broadly at the station in Shiprock.

'Lieutenant?'

'What?'

'You wanna clue?'

Tom Katon smiled and stuffed the radio back into its cradle. Just because he spent half his time with his nose in a book, John Henio thought he was smart, which in some ways he was. Except with people. He knew capitals and the names of the stars in the sky but he didn't know people. He couldn't read them. Tom Katon could. Like now. He could tell just by looking that the old man sitting on the step outside the Chai house was in some way real unusual, though he couldn't for the moment think why. For the moment he just pulled up outside the store and fetched his hat from the back seat. He put on his shades and crossed the dusty street.

'You Ethan Pierce?'

The old man said nothing.

'You okay?'

He nodded. He was sitting on his hands like a boy. 'The kid got hit,' he said.

'Bad?'

He shrugged.

'Did you see the driver?'

He shook his head.

'How about the car?'

He looked up. 'What?' His face was white despite the fierce sun, like it was drained of blood.

Tom Katon dipped down on his haunches.

'You sure you're okay?'

'I seen it,' said Ethan.

'The car?'

'Yellow it was.'

'Arizona plates?'

He shrugged.

Tom Katon fumbled through his pockets. He pulled out a pack of Lucky Strikes and passed them over. Ethan Pierce took one. His thin hands were shaking.

'You see the doctor?'

He cupped his boney fingers round the flame.

'I'm okay,' he said, though he plainly was not, 'I'm just a little shook up.'

Tom Katon drew hard on his cigarette. Giving up smoking was like fixing breakfast: too much to manage on his own. He squinted through the smoke. 'So were you headed east or west?'

'East. I guess.'

'Albuquerque?'

Ethan shrugged. 'I guess. The kid was driving. It was his trip. I was just hitching a ride.'

'Where're you from?'

Ethan shrugged again. 'Does it matter?'

'It might. Anyway, what about the girl?'

'I don't know.'

'You didn't know her?'

'No, sir. She's his girlfriend. Leastways she says she is.'

'You don't think so?'

Ethan Pierce looked up. 'I don't know, do I? Why you asking?'

'No reason.'

Tom Katon ground his cigarette butt into the dirt. He looked again at Ethan. The old man's hair was wild like the hair of Laver Tickel's boy over in Pica County who'd hanged himself on the overhead lines, Christmas Day 1975. He stood up.

'You reckon he'll be okay?' said Ethan.

Tom Katon smiled. 'Can't say,' he said. He turned and walked away.

It was cool in the Chai house. He removed his hat. A TV was flickering in the corner, its clean black newness out of place against the mud-baked walls and low-beamed ceiling. A small dark girl was lying wrapped in a bright-colored blanket on the couch, following the exploits of Wiley Coyote.

'Hi, Mr Katon,' she said without looking up from the TV.

'Hi, Rosie. You seen Agnes?'

'She left.'

'And your mama?'

Rosie Chai shook her head.

Tom Katon crossed to the window and looked out. The old man was still sitting on the step. He looked up from the dirt at the sound of a car.

'Mr Katon?'

'Yes, Rosie?'

'Are you gonna arrest them?'

'Arrest them? Why would I wanna do that?'

Rosie shrugged, she thought they were weird, the woman especially, the way she kept holding the sleeping man's hand and talking to him like he was awake.

A car pulled up outside.

Tom Katon bit his lip. 'Rosie?'

'What?'

'Did your mama say anything?'

On screen, Wiley Coyote was lighting a fuse attached to a black ball marked BOMB.

'She said you shouldn't of. She said you should be out catching robbers, not buying flowers. I reckon she was glad you did, though.'

'She said so?'

Outside a car door slammed.

'Mr Katon?'

'What?'

Rosie Chai looked up from the TV. 'Are you gonna ask mama again?'

Tom Katon said nothing. There were footsteps at the door. He cleared his throat and straightened his tie.

25

WANDA CHAI WAS the only woman Tom Katon could ever marry: he'd known this the first moment he'd seen her. Although she wasn't beautiful like Agnes was beautiful and she had a tongue on her sometimes that could make a man shiver, there was something about her that made the palms of his hands go clammy when he saw her and his words dry up like Old Man's Creek at the first sign of summer.

He licked his lips, shifting his weight from one foot to the other. 'Yaa eh teeh, Wanda.'

Wanda Chai set her bag in the corner. The jewelry inside chinked like coins. She closed the door. 'Well, flowerman,' she said. She was frowning, though behind the frown was a smile, like the sun behind clouds. 'I suppose you've come to collect.'

'Collect?'

'For the flowers.'

Tom Katon felt a heat rising up from the soles of his feet. 'They were a present, Wanda. You know they were a present.'

Wanda Chai shrugged and swayed across the room. At three hundred pounds she was as graceful in flow as a rolling river. She knelt at the couch. She touched Rosie's forehead with the back of her hand.

'Mama?'

'How're you feeling now?'

'Okay. Mama?'

'Yes?'

'Mr Katon wants to ask you a question. Don't you, Mr Katon?'

'Oh?' Without turning her dark head, without disturbing the fall of her blue-black hair, without lifting her hand from her daughter's brow, Wanda Chai said, 'And what could that be?'

'He wants to ask you to marry him, of course.'

'Does he?'

'Don't you, Mr Katon?'

Now she turned, she was smiling that smile. 'Is that right, Mr Katon?'

'Well –'

'Go on,' said Rosie impatiently.

'Ssh,' said Wanda. She pushed herself up. 'What's that?'

'What?' said Tom. His heart was thudding.

From the backroom came the sound of a woman singing, low like a lullaby.

'It's that weird woman,' huffed Rosie.

'What woman?'

'And a man. *He's* dead.'

Tom sighed. 'He ain't dead.'

'Well, nearly.'

'He was in an accident on the highway. Hit and run. Jimmy brought him in. He needed help. Look, Wanda –'

'Who is he?'

'Just some kid.'

'He'll be alright?'

'He'll be fine.'

'Has Agnes been by?'

Tom Katon nodded. He swallowed hard. He looked down at his dusty boots, he had a sense suddenly that this was his chance, maybe his last, who knows? 'Wanda?' He gripped his hat, turning it through his hands. Three times he'd asked her to marry him and three times she'd said maybe, I'll have to ask Father, and three times old Clarence had said no. He drew a breath. 'Well, I was wondering,' he said, looking up from his boots. 'Wanda?'

'Too late,' said Rosie with a sigh. There was talking now – women's voices – coming from the backroom. Rosie Chai shook her head slowly. Grown-ups, she thought, turning back to the TV. Hopeless.

26

TOM KATON TOOK the back way out of the Pueblo and headed east along the desert tracks in the general direction of the highway. He was in no hurry to get back to Shiprock and his paperwork, nor to get home where nothing but solitude was waiting. So, when the Pueblo dipped down in his mirror below the horizon he switched off his two-way radio and slowed the patrol car. The car rose and fell on the uneven ground. He let the wheel slip lazily through his hands. Sometimes there seemed no point in hurrying. Sometimes – however hard he tried – there were some things he never seemed able to change.

He wound down the window and let the breeze cool his face. The day so far was a failure: questions unanswered. The woman had seen no more of the car that had hit them than the old man, and the boy was still sleeping when he left, as still as a boy in a coma. And Wanda? Well she'd left without saying a word, taking Rosie for her treatment to the hospital in Gallup. He'd sat for a while watching TV and fiddling with his hat, half-listening to the Chai boys laughing and talking and hammering their silver in the workshop next door. The sound of their youth had made him feel about a hundred years old.

He turned left at the old quarry. Up ahead on the track a half-dozen black-coated ravens were feasting on the corpse of a prairie-dog. They rose as the car passed by, settling back when it'd gone. He took out a cigarette and pushed in the lighter. He tried not to think about Wanda.

Everybody knew they were made for each other, and everybody knew that if it weren't for Clarence then Wanda would stop saying maybe and start saying yes and then she and Tom would get married right away and that at last – at long long last

– would be that. Everybody knew this – especially Clarence. All day every day he sat out back in his old GI jacket and forage cap, cooling himself in the shade of the lean-to, just waiting (or so it seemed to Tom) for the chance to scupper another man's future and so secure his own in the cooking and housekeeping line. He was an obstacle that Tom had so far failed miserably to get around, though not for the want of trying. How many times had he sat out back listening again and again to stories of the D-Day landings? How many hours had he wasted nodding and smiling while the old man went on and on, his blinded eyes oblivious to the failing of the light? Too many – and for what? For nothing. He was no nearer marriage now than he'd ever been, though he *was* nearer fifty. At thirty-five he'd had years to spare; now, more and more – especially in the two years he'd known Wanda – he had a sense of time running out.

It was after four when he reached the highway. Slowing the car he changed down and drew up onto the road. The road was clear either way. He switched on his radio. It crackled impatiently.

'Lieutenant?'

He touched the button. John Henio sounded worried.

'You okay, Johnny?'

'I been trying to call. You okay?'

'Sure I'm okay. Why?'

The line crackled.

'Johnny?'

'You sure you're okay?'

'Positive.'

'And you ain't being followed?'

'No, I ain't being followed. What's going on?' Tom glanced in his mirror. Miles back, a truck was weaving through the heat.

'Johnny?'

'Some guy called.'

'What guy?'

'I don't know. Stevie took the call.'

'So?'

John Henio paused.

'Johnny?'

'He said, well, that you were dead.'

'What?'

'He said he'd killed you.'

Tom Katon touched the button. 'Well, he hasn't, Johnny. As you can hear.'

'But he said —'

'Take it easy, will you? He's just some crank. Some knight of the Order of Dipshit. They see an Indian in a uniform and they go crazy. It's their worst nightmare come alive. It don't mean nothing. 'Cept another dime for the phone company.'

'Well —'

'Well nothing, Johnny. Hey — you know what?'

'What?'

'You wanna hear something?'

'What?'

'Bogota,' said Tom Katon. 'The capital of Peru — right?'

'Right,' said John Henio, though he knew it wasn't, he couldn't think straight.

'Johnny?'

'Sure, Lieutenant.'

'Johnny?'

'What?'

'Take it easy, okay?'

'Okay, Lieutenant.'

Tom Katon clipped the radio back onto the dash. Despite his education — three years at Arizona State — John Henio still had a lot to learn — how to pick out the weirdos, for one thing, from the general parade of distressed humanity, and for another how to do it without getting spooked.

The blast of a trucker's horn split the air. Tom looked in his mirror. Slicker Skeety was smiling at the wheel of his sixteen-wheeler, his cap tipped back on his walnut head. He pulled out and passed, blasting his horn again and waving as he did so. Tom watched him go. The truck rose steadily with the rising road, its flanks gleaming sharp in the sun. He watched it until it was gone from sight. Then he re-tuned the radio and listened to the incoming calls.

He was two miles out of Yellow Springs when something – a shape in the desert – caught his eye. He pulled over and got out of the car. There were tire tracks leading down off the highway and over the scrub. They stopped at what looked like the roof of a car. He shaded his eyes and looked around. The road and the desert were empty. 'Hello?' he called. Nothing. Holding onto his gun, he slithered down the bank.

The car was a bright yellow 73 Toyota, buried to its windshield in the sand. The driver's door had been forced open a foot or so. Tom Katon peered inside. The car was empty, the radio on but knocked off-station. He reached over and turned it off. His hand brushed the wheel. The wheel was wet with blood.

27

WITH THE DAY drifting on towards dusk, Clarence Chai watched the figure making its way across the fields of water-melon. The figure – dressed in a black coat and broad-brimmed preacher's hat – was moving slowly, swerving like an injured person or someone dazed from a recent accident. He stumbled sometimes and sometimes fell and lay where he fell as still in the fields as a corpse. Now and then he stopped and tipped back his head like a farmer praying for rain; other times he just looked down at his shoes for minutes on end, for all the world like a mourner looking down upon a grave.

Clarence Chai stetched his fingers. Trouble, he thought, though he didn't stir. He just sat watching, every now and then blinking, every now and then starting his chair on a gentle rocking motion. He squinted, watching the figure moving on then stumbling. Trouble, he thought. But not a blindman's trouble. He stretched his fingers again, testing the unwilling joints. He pushed from the knees and rocked some more.

He'd been sitting in the yard since early morning (as he did every morning, often staying well into the night) as usual just rocking and thinking – letting his thoughts drift over him – when his eye had caught the figure moving slowly far off through the rippling heat of the desert. Dark against the sun then darker still as he'd moved through the shadow of Blue Mesa, the figure had had a strangeness about him even at a distance, his pale face and hands, so pale against his clothes, giving him the feverish look of a soul prone to madness. Even at a distance his look had spelled trouble. Even to a blindman like Clarence.

The figure stopped abruptly. Clarence squinted. The figure stood a moment swaying like a drunk, then moved on. Clarence flexed his fingers, watching. He listened to the voices and the babbling of the TV in the house and he thought again about Wanda and how when she knew his special secret she'd be mad. He shielded his eyes. For a moment the figure was out of sight behind the latrine, but then he appeared again, swaying still and stumbling and kicking up dust from his heels. He lurched and fell and lay where he fell. Clarence squinted hard through the dusk-light. Beyond the fields and the scrub, beyond the pylons that bordered the highway, the mountains were fading to blackness. Soon, only the oat-colored moon and Clarence — old blind Clarence — were watching.

It wasn't that he didn't like Tom Katon. Tom Katon was a decent enough man, and above average in politeness if the way he sat and listened was anything to go by. No, it wasn't Tom Katon he didn't like, nor the others before him: it was what his presence meant that Clarence didn't like. He and the others before him meant a daughter married and gone away and an old helpless man left on his own with only his thoughts and the kindness of strangers to rely on, and although Wanda had said she'd never leave him there'd always been a chance, people — even Wanda — being what people are.

He shifted in his chair. A voice — Wanda's — rose up from the house, filling him with dread. What would she say when she found out? He didn't dare think of it. She'd be mad: that much was certain. She'd walk out for sure, and take Jimmy and the other boys with her and he'd never see her or them again.

I'll tell her, he thought. Right now. He turned to call her, but the impulse shrank away. What could he say? How could he tell her that he wasn't blind at all any more — that for a year and a half now his sight had step by step been returning, and that far from being blind now he could make out the features of a stranger still a mile or more away? She'd get mad for sure however he said it, and that would be that. He flexed his fingers. Maybe later, he thought. He stared out into the darkness. He listened gloomily to the hum of the desert.

It was after midnight when he woke.

'Father?'

It was Wanda. She'd been in his dream, packing her bags and slamming doors.

'Are you all right? Aren't you cold?'

Tell her, said a voice.

He shrugged.

Tell her.

'I thought I heard someone,' he said. 'Out there.' He pointed vaguely, blindly out towards the dark vermilion fields.

'Come on,' said Wanda. She put her arm through his and started lifting.

'Wanda?'

'Yes?'

Tell her.

In his dream she'd been crying, her face streaming tears.

'What is it?'

He heaved himself up. 'Nothing,' he said.

28

NIGHT IN THE DESERT. A world of sleep and death. In the cottonwoods beyond the highway a horned owl gathered himself, cool on his perch, while cactus wrens and morning doves returned to their nests in spikey chollas. In the mesquite, a silver-grey coyote sniffed for mice and kaibab ground squirrels, and a long-nosed snake took fifteen minutes to swallow the stiffening corpse of a rat. Lizards scurried; a scorpion paralyzed its victim. A warm breeze, last breath of day, drifted over the desert, ruffling the cottonwoods and waxen junipers. All seemed still, but was not still. All was livid, scratching and uncoiling in the darkness of inverted day.

Ethan Pierce turned again on the couch. He couldn't sleep. There was a terrible restlessness in his old limbs. He lay awhile squinting at the darkness. He listened to the sleeping sounds of the house.

It was a strange thing but, since his illness, both his memory and his grip on the past had loosened. Where once sleeplessness would have brought forth the faces of those who'd disappointed or annoyed him — Mr Squire at the Elevator Company, for instance, or the punk at the gas station back in sixty-eight who'd called him Hopeless Joe just because he'd hung around demanding his free set of steak knives, or the son who'd abandoned him — where once they'd have crowded in, raising his blood pressure and making him feel as mad as he knew he'd a right to be, now there was nothing: it was as if a blackboard had been wiped clean, as if something or someone (for this is truly how it felt) were saying never look back, always look forward, and as if, in order that he should do this, that someone had filled him with the energy and hope for the future that he'd hardly even known as a child. Indeed, these nights since the illness he'd felt truly energized and unable to sleep. He stared into the darkness, wondering. These nights he could barely wait for the dawn. These days the days never came soon enough.

In a while he pushed himself up. He crossed the floor and eased open the front door. Outside the night was humming, the sky overhead blue-black and filled with a million stars. He pulled the door to and made his way along the dusty moonlit tracks, raising dust at his heels, out beyond the dwellings to where the desert began. He leaned on the rail of a sheep-pen and gazed out towards the mountains. There were lights moving slow on the Interstate, east and west, and the lights of a plane dipping down beyond the mountains on the run-in to Phoenix. Ethan settled his chin in his hands, watching. It was amazing, now he came to think of it, just how many people there are in the world, each living their separate lives – some being born, others dying, some getting married, others heading out to a bar or the movies with just a few dollars or pesos or yen in their pockets. Millions, he thought, maybe millions of millions, none of whom knew about him and none of whom he knew. It was enough, when he thought about it, to make him feel awful lonesome and make him wonder if what a person does, good or bad, however hard he tries, however successful he is, can really amount to anything at all and whether it wouldn't just be better to expect nothing from life but at best the painless passage of time and so not be disappointed.

The sheep in the dark pen rustled, huddling, as a breeze blew over the desert bringing with it the faraway howl of a hungry coyote. Ethan stared at the shapes in the darkness, his heart growing suddenly heavy with the night. He moved away, scuffing his boots as he walked, not lifting his head, thinking once more of the past he'd thought had receded. He felt suddenly his age again and suddenly – every minute – a minute closer to oblivion. The darkness seemed to bustle and jostle him as he walked. He hurried on. He had the sense suddenly of eyes upon him. It was the lost years watching him: he knew this. He pushed on the door of the Chai house and crossed the floor and sat heavily on the couch. He hung his head. It was enough sometimes to make a man wish he was dead.

It was three o'clock when a car bumped down the track, its lights flaring then passing on. In a moment the sound of its engine was gone and silence returned. Ethan wiped the tears from his cheeks. He felt himself sitting on something hard. He reached underneath himself and pulled out a TV remote. He squinted at it in the gloom.

In his book *Acts Of God* (*How The Lord Shows His Hand*), Emerson E. Gardner records the following:

At that moment, without a button being pressed, the TV flicked on and Ethan Pierce, his cheeks still wet with tears of emptiness, was faced with the smiling piety of the Reverend Jimmy Swaggert. But not for long. For no sooner had he focused his ageing eyes on the Reverend's smooth features, than the image was replaced by another, then another. The TV, it seemed, just by the old man's touch, was suddenly a mad thing, hopping like a rabbit from station to station, buzzing and crackling as if it were alive with untold energies . . .

Ethan dropped the remote. The TV clicked off. He stared at it for a moment, then gingerly picked it up. '. . . is on offer to you,' said a voice at once from the TV, followed by a picture, 'for only thirty-nine dollars and ninety-nine cents . . .' He dropped it again. Again, silence. He stared at the remote lying on the matting floor. He stared at his hand, turning it over. 'Jesus,' he whispered. He stared at the TV. The dawn was rising, lighting the room. He could see himself in the TV glass, white-faced, staring back.

And so could Jubal Early. Jubal Early, his head still thumping from his crash, stepped away from the window. He pulled out his notebook, his pen. He stood for a moment, thinking. Then, his thinking done, he opened the notebook and started writing.

29

WHEN HE WOKE next morning in Wanda Chai's bed, Perry Jemson felt like a boxer the morning after a losing fight. His limbs were heavy, his head pounding. How long he'd been sleeping he couldn't have said, though it seemed like days. He tried to sit up but the pain in his head forced him back. He gazed around the room. The room was dark, curtains drawn against the day. He let his eyes close. He tried to remember what had happened.

There was a pick-up: he remembered that. He remembered also standing by a roadside, then turning at the sound of a car. Then there was nothing.

'Yaa eh teeh,' said a voice.

He opened his eyes.

'You've had a long sleep.'

He squinted. The face of a woman loomed through the gloom. She was an Indian, dark-skinned, bright-eyed.

'How're you feeling?' she said.

He licked his lips. They were dry and cracked.

'What happened?'

Wanda Chai smiled. 'You had an accident, but now you're alright.'

'Accident?'

She touched Perry's hand. 'On the highway.'

And then he remembered. He remembered all at once Marla and Ethan Pierce and the whole absurd shambles of his getaway.

'Are you thirsty?' said Wanda.

Perry nodded. By now, Philly would be frantic. By now he'd have searched the whole town, his panic growing wilder by the minute. By now anything could have happened. Perry tried not to think of it.

Wanda Chai left the room. In a while Perry pushed himself up. There was a rattling fan turning slow on the far wall. Clenching his teeth against the pain he forced his legs around and set his feet on the floor. He made his way slowly step by step across the floor.

Ethan Pierce was sitting on an upturned soda crate across the track in the shade of the store. Beside him was a large empty barrel. He was drawing shapes in the sand with a stick. He looked up at the sound of a screen door banging, shielding his eyes from the sun.

'Hey, kid!'

Perry crossed the track and lowered himself onto the stoop. He rubbed his temples.

'You okay, kid?'

'Where is this place?'

'Santo Doringo,' said Ethan.

'Where?'

'On the Reservation.'

'Jesus,' said Perry. 'How long was I out?'

Ethan shrugged. 'About a day. You sure you're okay? Me and Marla was awful worried –'

'I said I'm okay,' said Perry. He shuffled back on the stoop, out of the sun. The sun was burning. It was midday.

Wanda brought them water-melon and two chequered napkins. They sat and ate the moist flesh in silence, spitting the seeds out onto the dirt, just watching the folks come and go.

After a while, Ethan said, 'Hey, kid, you know about electricity?'

Perry was gazing down the street, watching Agnes crouched down on a step, her practised fingers moving through the hair on the back of a small boy's head.

'Kid?'

'Don't call me kid.'

'Sorry, kid.' Ethan paused. Agnes moved on. 'Well do you?'

'Do I what?'

'Know anything 'bout electricity. How it can jump around and stuff.'

Perry turned his head. His head felt tight, like there were hands pressing in. 'Jump around? What do you mean jump around?'

'Like from, say, a TV to a person maybe?'

Perry sighed. In the eye of his mind he saw his brother curled up in a corner someplace, his knees drawn up tight and his hands held for fear across his eyes.

'Kid?'

'What?'

'Well, do you think it can?'

'What?'

'Electricity. Jump around.'

'Maybe. I don't know.' Perry shrugged. 'I guess not.'

'No,' said Ethan. 'Course not. That's what I reckoned.'

They sat again in silence. Again, Ethan was the first to speak.

'Hey, kid, you know what?'

'What?'

'I was thinking. About our trip.'

Perry turned, he felt suddenly so weary. '*Our* trip?'

'Sure. You, me and Marla.'

'Jesus,' he said.

'What is it?'

'What is it? What do you mean what is it? What it is is in the first place this ain't no trip, and in the second place if it's anybody's trip it sure as hell ain't your trip, okay?'

'Hey, okay –'

'And in the third place –' Suddenly Perry couldn't think of a third place. He pushed himself up. His head seemed to swerve. Like water pouring through a cracked drain, Philly slipped into his mind again. By now Philly would know that Perry wasn't coming back. By now he'd know he was all alone.

A hand touched Perry's thigh, stinging. He jumped.

'Kid?'

He got up, moved away across the track. He had to get away – from Bagdad, from the state, from Philly, from everything. If he didn't, then pretty soon he'd find himself stuck and getting old, unable to move then even if he wanted to.

He crossed to the Chai house. It was cool inside. Rosie Chai was stretched out on the couch in front of the TV. From the corner of her eye she watched Perry go into the backroom. There were shuffling sounds. He came out carrying a sports bag. He started back across the room but then stopped. He said, 'Do you know where they put my pick-up?'

Rosie Chai stared hard at the TV.

'Did you hear me?'

Never talk to strangers her mama always said, and this man was strange. She clenched her teeth.

'Well?'

She could feel herself flushing. She stared hard at the Roadrunner, excluding all else. Hopeful as ever, Wiley Coyote lit a fuse. She narrowed her eyes. In a moment Perry Jemson moved out of sight. The screen door banged behind him.

Ethan Pierce was still sitting on his soda crate, leaning against the large empty barrel.

'Hey, kid — you okay?'

Perry shielded his eyes. The sun was fierce. 'You seen my pick-up?' he said.

Ethan Pierce shrugged. He pushed himself up, hands on his boney knees. 'We leaving now?'

Perry Jemson shook his head. '*We* ain't,' he said, turning away.

He found the pick-up parked on the edge of the Pueblo at the point where the Pueblo drifts back into desert and the land begins its slow shallow dip down across the plains to the mountains. Beside it in the sand lay the wingless husk of an old two-engine Dakota, preserved for nearly half a century rust-free in the warm dry air.

Perry tossed his bag in the back of the pick-up and got in. He held the key in the ignition a moment, his eyes closed in silent bargaining with the Great God of Motors.

He pressed the gas.

Come on.

He turned the key.

Nothing.

He turned it again.

Come on, come on.

Click.

And again, again.

Click, click.

'You'll flood it,' said Jimmy Chai.

Perry turned sharply.

Jimmy Chai was sitting up in the nose of the Dakota, his chin on his arms and his arms on the rim of the pilot's now-glassless window. His face was smooth and as brown as dark leather. His teeth shone white when he smiled.

'Something funny?' said Perry.

Jimmy Chai shrugged. The clicking of the motor had raised him from sleep. He'd been dreaming as always of flying the world – India, Africa, across the frozen Arctic.

'It's your battery,' he said.

'I know.'

'Sounds dead.'

'I *know*.'

Perry turned the key again. Still nothing.

'You'll flood it,' said Jimmy Chai.

'I can't flood it if I can't start it, can I?'

'If you say so.'

Perry tried the engine once more, then gave up. He slumped back in the seat. Philly appeared again, this time collapsed in the yard back home as he'd been once before. He pushed the image away. He sat up. 'Is there someone who can charge it?' he said.

'There's Charlie Houck.'

'Would he have a spare one? Is he a mechanic?'

Jimmy Chai nodded.

'Is he here?'

'Nope. Kayenta. But he'll be here tomorrow. He always comes Tuesdays. Are you in a hurry?'

Perry said nothing. He could feel invisible fingers tugging him, back, back.

'Hey, look,' said Jimmy Chai.

'What?'

'It's your friend.'

Ethan Pierce was advancing through the dust, waving his arms.

'Hey, kid – thank the Lord I found you! Have we got trouble!'

Perry shrank back down behind the wheel. 'Oh God,' he said. He covered his face.

It turned out Jimmy Chai wasn't the only one who'd been dreaming that day. So had Marla – and not pleasant dreams neither. Exhausted from her all-night vigil (she'd determined to be there if Perry had woken in the night), she'd fallen asleep on Wanda's kingsize, straight into the arms of a nightmare. She'd dreamed she was standing alone in the desert, surrounded by ever-encroaching car-sized scorpions and snakes as long as Silverman's Creek. She'd screamed at the first bite and her screams had woken her. According to Ethan Pierce she was screaming still.

Perry shook his head. 'So what the hell am I supposed to do about it?'

'She's asking for you, kid. When she ain't screaming, that is. She says –' Ethan paused. He moved nearer, up to the pick-up's window. He lowered his voice. 'She says if you don't go see her, well, she's gonna kill herself –'

'What?'

'Says she's gonna die for love –'

'She says she's gonna *what*?'

'You better go, kid –'

Perry shook his head. 'I ain't going no place.'

'But Marla said –'

'To hell with Marla.'

'But –'

'I said to hell with her – okay?'

'You don't mean that, kid. You can't –'

'Can't I? Can't I? Watch me.' Forgetting, Perry twisted the pick-up's key. The motor clicked insolently. He slammed the wheel.

'Easy, kid.'

'Don't call me kid!'

106

'Sorry, kid.' Ethan paused. 'Kid?'

Perry said nothing.

'Look, kid, I know how you feel –'

Perry turned sharp. 'Oh?'

'But if it were my girl, well –' Ethan shrugged.

'Hold it,' said Perry. 'She ain't my girl.'

'She ain't?'

'No. She ain't.'

Ethan frowned. 'You mean you ain't getting married?'

'What?'

'And you ain't gonna visit with your sister in Buffalo as a sort of honeymoon, seeing as how you can't afford a proper honeymoon yet what with all the expense of a house and Perry Junior being on the way and all?'

'No,' said Perry.

'Sweet Jesus.' Ethan blew out his cheeks. 'Have we got trouble.'

'We?' Perry shook his head. 'I ain't got trouble.'

'But she's asking for you, kid. She says only you can stop her –'

'Killing herself?' Perry snorted.

'Drowning herself.'

'Drowning? Here? In the middle of the Goddamn desert?'

Ethan shook his head. 'She's talking about a dam. Says she's gonna throw herself in –'

'Oh? And what dam would that be?'

Ethan shrugged. 'Boulder, I guess. She didn't specify. Kid, I really think she means it –'

'She don't mean it.'

'She do!'

'Bullshit!'

Again, Perry turned the key, then again, again. He slammed the dash.

'Hey, steady, kid –' Ethan gripped the door's metal frame. Perry turned the key again. This time, like a miracle, the spark plugs fired and the motor turned over, better now than it ever had.

'Yes,' hissed Perry. He gunned the engine. *Go*, said a voice in his head, *Go*. He dropped the handbrake. He paused a moment. Ethan Pierce was looking, startled, at his hands. Perry studied the old man's face. 'Hey, Ethan,' he said.

Ethan said nothing. His hands were tingling: pins and needles.

'I gotta go, Ethan. Ethan?'

Ethan looked up.

'You'll be okay, Ethan. And Marla. You'll get a ride. Okay? Ethan?'

Ethan heard himself saying okay. He watched the pick-up pull away. It bumped across the uneven ground, down the narrow alleyway between the low sand-colored dwellings. The engine raved a moment, hanging in the warm air, then at last it grew quieter, then was gone.

Four

30

THE DAY WAS DRAGGING slow for Jimmy Chai. It seemed as if time had slowed down or even stopped. He looked again at the workshop clock. Two-fifteen. Every time he looked at the clock which was every few minutes he expected hours to have passed, though they never had. He looked down again at his work. His fingers knew the work so well – threading beads, working silver into shape, polishing the turquoise and malachite till it shone – that he hardly had to think, just let his fingers run like the parts of a machine, minute after minute, hour after hour, day after day. Most days he pretended he wasn't there at all. Most days in his mind he was flying.

What it was about flying that so appealed to him, Jimmy Chai couldn't really have said, although if asked (which he never had been) he'd probably have said, *Being up there looking down.* In his daydreams and in his dreams at night, he imagined looking down at the desert and cities and the ocean, just watching the people going on about their business and the cars on the highway like toy cars, all the time seeing but being unseen, all the time moving on, over, the only sign of his being there at all a fleeting shadow on the earth.

The radio in the window drifted off station again. It was an old radio and seemed unable to concentrate. Jimmy put down his work and crossed the room to re-tune it. The tuning knob was loose and you had to turn it and turn it to make much progress on the dial. The tiny speaker crackled and buzzed as it neared a station. Jimmy slowed down his turning, easing it on. Far off, Holly Dunn drew nearer, her voice so sweet you could spread it on toast. *Oh, as long as you belong to me,* she sang. Jimmy stood a while listening, his eyes drifting up and down the Pueblo's dusty main street. As his fingers knew their work, so his eyes knew the Pueblo. He knew every dip in the road and the twist of every aerial and the line on every face so well that should it suddenly be he and not his grandfather who was blind nothing would really need to change: everything could go on just as it was – the same present, the same future, the same sun on his skin.

The store door opened across the street, the sound of its bell muffled in the heat. Agnes paused on the stoop and adjusted her hat. Jimmy watched her. Her hat was a wide-brimmed affair with a band of red silk. The silk matched the color of her dress which came, Jimmy knew, from a shop in the Coronado Mall in Albuquerque. The shop was called Barnaby's and sold clothes copied from those available in Europe or New York but at much reduced prices. Jimmy knew that's where she'd bought the dress because, three weeks ago, quite by chance, he'd watched her buy it. He'd been sitting in the window of McDonald's studying the pictures in *Aviation Week* (he'd been out on an errand buying tools – tiny pliers and hammers – from the Indian Depot on Mission Street) when he'd raised his eyes and there she was. She was looking in the window of the shop across the way, her head cocked to one side, studying the dress. He'd watched her pause then go inside, losing her then for a while amongst the people. Minutes had passed and he'd just started wondering if it had been her at all when sure enough she'd come out smiling and carrying a bag. That day, as he'd watched her walk away, he'd tried to imagine where she was going – tried to picture a house and a yard – but his mind had drawn nothing. It was stupid, he knew, but up until that moment he'd never thought of her as having another, other life – never imagined her existing outside of her twice-weekly visits to the Pueblo. That day, as he'd watched her, losing her finally in the crowds, Jimmy Chai had felt a part of his life knocked off-balance. He'd tried to go back to his magazine, but his will for it, for the moment, had gone. Instead he'd gazed out at the people in the Mall, suddenly aware of the vastness of their numbers and his own insignificance. That night he'd lain in his bed listening to the Pueblo's nightsounds, more certain than ever that if ever he was to amount to anything then he must get away and soon, must cut himself adrift from safe sterile harbor and chance himself on the uneven torrents of the world.

Holly Dunn quit singing. Jimmy stood a while longer gazing out at the street, then went back to his work. He watched his fingers twisting and turning the silver as he'd watched them a thousand times and more. On the radio, Steve Wariner was *Drivin' and Cryin'*: Jimmy listened to his tale of love and loss. More and more every day he felt the day coming when he'd just up and leave. He turned the pliers, twisting a hook into place. He'd planned it all in his mind and soon – any day now – he'd be gone. Any day now he'd be driving himself right up to the gates of the 57th Tactical Air Wing at Tucson and be signing on the line for service. Any day now: he just had to do it. He just had to quit thinking about it and do it. He laid the earrings ready for polishing on a tray and stretched his back, his fingers. He closed his eyes, just floating, as three o'clock came and went. He just had to walk away and keep walking. He just had to go. Simple as that.

He slipped out the back way when he heard his brothers coming and made his way through the quiet sleeping streets. He climbed into the shell of the old Dakota and laid down in the cool. He closed his eyes, exhausted by his plans, and was soon dreaming. In his dreams as ever he was flying high and clear, seeing but unseen, looking down upon the earth from the blue cloudless skies.

31

'SAY AAH.'

'What?'

'Say aah.'

'Aah.'

'Again.'

'Aaaah.'

Agnes narrowed her eyes and considered Ethan's tongue. That done, she looked in his ears. There was, she concluded, nothing wrong with him. Except age, that is. 'How old are you?' she said.

Ethan shrugged. For a day and a half he'd been asking for a doctor — insisting, in fact, wasn't going to budge till he saw one — but now he regretted it. *I think I'm electric*: it sounded now so foolish — the ravings of a lunatic or some senile old fool.

Agnes unclipped her stethoscope, folded it up and put it back in her bag. 'Seventy-nine?' she said. 'Eighty?'

Again Ethan shrugged.

'Don't you remember?'

'Look,' he said miserably. He gripped the bright-colored blanket. 'I made a mistake — alright?'

'A mistake?'

This time for sure Vern would find him and have him put away and he'd wind up in a home someplace playing checkers with the dead and watching *Psychic Friends Network*.

'Ethan?'

'I'm sorry,' he said.

'Sorry?'

'For bothering you. Like I say, I made a mistake.'

'What mistake would that be, Ethan?'

Ethan looked down at his hands.

'Your hands? What about them?'

'I thought —' He stopped himself: no point in repeating it. Besides she'd probably know anyway: they'd be sure to have told her, sure to have said, He thinks he's electric and we think he's mad —

'Ethan?'

'Nothing' he said. 'It was the heat.'

'Ah yes,' said Agnes. This seemed to satisfy her and she clipped the buckle of her bag and stood up. Smiling, she turned away, but then turned back. 'How old did you say you were?'

'Ninety-one,' he said, not thinking, and then he thought *Damn* and he forced up a smile. 'But I only feel sixty!'

'Of course.' Agnes turned away again, her body shifting like sand within the sheath of her dress. Again she paused. 'Wanda said something about a pick-up,' she said. 'Yours?'

Ethan shifted uncomfortably in the bed, aware for the first time in two decades of activity in his shorts.

'Ethan?'

He swallowed hard. 'Yes?'

Agnes frowned. 'Are you okay? You look hot suddenly.'

'I'm fine.'

'Sure?'

Ethan nodded. He could feel a tide rising through his chest. His head he felt sure any minute would be flashing like a beacon.

Agnes studied him a moment. 'Anyway,' she said. 'That pick-up. Wanda says you've been pushing it. To get it started. Is this true?'

Ethan shook his head.

'No?'

From its hiding-place years back, the image of his wife came suddenly to him. She was standing in her night-dress, shaking her head. He winced.

'Ethan?'

'I'm sorry,' he said.

'Sorry? What for now?'

He shrugged. He looked down at his hands. Beneath them,

beneath the blanket, the rising had subsided. His wife drifted off, as if into a crowd.

'Ethan?'

He looked up.

'You must be careful, you know. Being an older person.'

'Okay,' said Ethan.

'No push-starting pick-ups, okay?'

But I didn't, he wanted to say, I just put my hands on the door and Bingo! But he didn't: it seemed now too absurd and probably untrue.

'Good,' said Agnes, as if something and not nothing had been resolved. She touched Ethan's foot through the blanket. She smiled and said something that Ethan didn't catch. He watched her leave the room, the door shutting behind her. An enormous weariness lay heavy on his old limbs and he laid down the weight of his head. It occurred to him then as he stared up at the ceiling-beams that he might never move again, might never get the chance to make amends, and that maybe the weight of his failures had at last found him out, and that here in the desert beneath the eyes of coyotes he'd be laid to his rest in an unquiet unmourned grave.

32

OFFICER STEVIE NEZ folded his copy of the *Navajo Times* and laid it on his desk. He stretched back in his chair and gazed around the squad room. Despite the presence of three other officers the room was quiet. It mostly was around four o'clock. Four o'clock on the Big Res was criminal down-time: that window of relative calm between the offences (fighting mostly) incited by lunch-hour drinking and those incited by the drinking done at night.

He got up and crossed to the window. Main Street was quiet too. He watched the lights change outside BigaBite Burgers and a car turn lazily away onto Sun Street. The car was a beat-up Firebird belonging to Frankie Platero, the rasp of its silencer the only sound in the thick air. It moved slow through the heat off the road, disappearing for a moment behind the Savings and Loan, then reappearing on the bridge across the San Juan River. The river was thick-brown, barely moving. The Firebird turned left on sixty-four, heading for Teec Nos Pos and Mexican Water. Stevie Nez squinted. Everyone knew Frankie Platero was a bum and always up to something. Just like his brother Luke. Together, as youngsters, they'd had a thing about ripping the chrome off cars, even though they couldn't sell it and trying to was how they'd got caught. Later they'd graduated to stealing the cars themselves, and later still to the state penitentiary on an eighteen-month stretch for aggravated burglary. Despite this (or perhaps because of it) Frankie Platero was always smiling – known for it – as if he knew something that no one else knew, or as if, whatever was done to him, he just didn't care. You got the feeling that even if you shot him (and plenty of people wished someone would) he'd just go on smiling, even into the mortuary and out the other side. He had a look that made you want to look away. It was the look of a person without a conscience. The look of a person that nothing could save.

Stevie Nez turned away from the window. 'Hey, either of you guys seen Luke?' he said.

Bruce Lasalu looked up. The oldest of the three (John Henio – the youngest – was kneeling in front of the coffee machine trying to retrieve a stuck quarter with a screwdriver), he stared a minute like he was thinking then shrugged and went back to his paperwork. Way past an age when he should have made Lieutenant, Bruce Lasalu was as zealous now in avoiding engagement as once he'd been in courting it.

'Hey, Johnny, how about you?'

John Henio gave a final rough stab with the screwdriver. The quarter wouldn't budge. He slammed the machine with the side of his foot.

'What?'

'Luke Platero.'

'What about him?'

'Have you seen him?'

John Henio, twenty-three, three years younger than Stevie Nez, was sitting on the edge of his desk nursing his instep. 'Yeah, I seen him,' he said.

'Where?'

He stopped rubbing his foot a second. 'Down at the Trails I think. Yeah. With that knucklehead brother of his.'

'What were they doing?'

'Nothing.' John Henio shrugged. 'Just hanging out. Why?'

'No reason.'

The telephone rang on Bruce Lasalu's desk. He ignored it.

'Hey, Brucie.'

John Henio smiled and winked at Stevie Nez. Bruce Lasalu just turned his page and went on writing.

'Ain't you gonna answer it? Could be that girlfriend of yours – what's her name? Annie? Aggie?'

Bruce Lasalu turned a page.

'Could be a hot date, Brucie. You don't wanna miss out now, do you Brucie?'

Without looking up, Bruce Lasalu lifted the receiver and put it straight back down. The ringing stopped.

'Shut it, shithead,' he said.

John Henio beamed. 'Hey! That's not nice!' He grinned at Stevie Nez, but Stevie Nez wasn't playing. Stevie Nez was thinking about Luke and Frankie and the Navajo Trails Motel.

The call came at five. Alone in the office, Stevie Nez drew a breath and lifted the receiver.

'Yes?'

It was always five o'clock. For three days now, on the stroke of the hour, the same voice, the same message – *He's dead, you know, that Katon* – the same sound of dogs in the background.

'Who is this?'

'It's me.'

The breath left his body as if he'd been punched. 'Jesus Christ, Lucy, what the hell're you doing?'

'Doing? I'm calling you up. What do you think I'm doing?'

Stevie Nez slumped back in his chair. There was sweat on his hair-line. He wiped it with the back of his hand.

'Stevie? Are you okay?'

'Yeah, I'm fine,' he said. 'I thought you were someone else.'

'Who else?'

'Just someone.'

A pause.

'A *work* someone, Lucy.'

Another pause.

'Lucy?'

'Okay.'

'I'm glad you called.'

'Are you?'

'You know it.' Stevie Nez changed the receiver hand to hand. He watched his spare hand flip the pages of his diary.

'Stevie?'

'Yes?'

'I was thinking. About you.'

'Me too. Favorite subject.'

119

'No, really thinking. About you and me. About us.'

About us. Here we go, thought Stevie. He braced himself.

'Stevie? Are you listening?'

'I'm listening.'

'Well, I was thinking. You know how you're always saying how one day you want to be a daddy?'

Stevie's hand froze.

'Stevie?'

'Go on.'

'And that if you ever found out you couldn't be you'd be real upset?'

'I remember.'

'Well –'

Lucy paused. There was breathing on the line, the faintest trace of distress.

'Lucy? What is it?'

'It's me.'

'What?'

'I saw the doctor.'

'What doctor?'

'What do you mean what doctor? Does it matter?'

'What're you saying?'

'What I'm saying is I saw the doctor and he said it's me. As can't have kids. Not now. Never.' There was a sudden defiance in Lucy's voice, a challenge. It was the prelude, Stevie knew, to a bout of bitter rage. He felt himself shrinking from it.

'Stevie? Did you hear me?'

He was staring at the window, at the grease marks on the glass. He'd a moment – one chance – to say the right thing. Absurdly, Frankie Platero popped into his head.

'Stevie?'

Frankie Platero was smiling, standing over a corpse.

'Stevie? Are you there?'

'I'm here.'

Silence. A crackle on the line.

'Stevie?'

He said, 'Are you sure?'

'Sure?'

It was the wrong thing: he knew it as soon as he heard the words. There was silence again, breathing.

'Lucy?'

A heavy breath.

'Lucy?'

'Oh, Stevie –'

Then the clunk of the tumbling receiver, then a buzzing, then nothing.

John Henio walked into the room. He was carrying two cups. He stopped, frowning. 'You okay? You look like shit.'

Stevie set down the receiver. It rang at once. He picked it up.

'Hi, Stevie.'

For a moment he was lost in a fog.

'I been waiting on you, Stevie. You and that girl of yours sure do a mess of talking –'

He squeezed his temples. 'What?'

Then the sound of barking dogs came distant down the line, blasting the fog.

'Stevie?'

He slammed down the receiver. His heart was pumping. *You and that girl of yours*. He stared at John Henio. John Henio stared back.

'Trouble?'

'Oh yeah,' said Stevie Nez. 'Oh yeah.'

33

TOM KATON SCANNED the desert. There was nothing to see but sand and scrub — miles of it, flat empty miles stretching out to the line of the sky. He lowered his binoculars and rubbed his eyes. All day he'd been searching, covering every inch from Williams to Kingman, but so far nothing. He turned and leaned on the roof of the car, scanning the other way. A roadrunner dashed into the circle of his sight, then away. He scanned a while longer, the dips and hollows of the land as it rose towards Blue Mesa then flattened out again to the mountains — but nothing. All day nothing. A day wasted. He lowered the binoculars and got back into the car.

He'd been nearing the Pueblo when the call had come in. A woman had been seen by a trucker wandering off the highway somewhere between Williams and Kingman. She'd looked on her last legs: could anyone deal? To start with he'd ignored it (he was off-duty for one thing and for another he had plans), but the longer he'd driven the worse he'd felt. What if the woman was hurt? What if she didn't know the desert and collapsed and died out there? He'd had to turn around and go look.

He pulled over a few miles up the road and got out. And he'd had such plans. He'd cleaned himself up (new shirt, tie) and the car too and worked himself up into a state so as he'd not take no for an answer and whatever Wanda said he'd just say Well, that's fine but this is the way it's gonna be and you're just gonna like it at least in time even if you don't like it now — he'd planned it all, but then the call had come in and his fool sense of duty had turned him around and here he was standing in the back end of nowhere looking for a woman who was either so dumb she deserved what she'd surely get or who didn't exist at all, being the imaginings of some lonesome old boy who saw women in the desert the way cold-turkey drunks see tequila in the bath. Either way, the day that had started with such promise and so early (he'd been up at five pressing his shirt and a clean pair of pants) was now drifting to nothing as days these days often seemed to do. These days, it seemed, he could plan all he liked but it wouldn't mean squat if Someone Up There didn't like it. And did they ever like it? No, sir. Not these days. These days, every day, it was Screw Katon Day.

He gripped the binoculars and swept Blue Mesa. Nothing. A few sweeps more and he abandoned his search. His head was pounding from staring into the sun and he was no longer in the mood for charity. He tossed the binoculars in the back of the car, dropped the brake and sped off. It was too late now for anything but home: a beer and a ballgame and the slow usual slide into night. He switched on the radio, but the cheery babbling voices depressed him. He switched it off. Instead he drove in silence, aware that every mile that passed was a mile nearer home but a mile further away from love and comfort and the arms of the woman he adored but now knew he'd lose. He knew now as he drove (how he knew he couldn't have said, but he knew) that he'd never again get a chance like today, that he'd never again have the courage and the means, and that from now on he'd better get used to solitude, for it was that which lay ahead as surely as the road and as surely and certainly as the grave.

He stopped for gas on the outskirts of Shiprock and was just sitting thinking nothing, drumming his fingers on the wheel, when a call came through on the radio. He let it buzz a while, then answered.

'Lieutenant?'

He sighed.

'You there, Lieutenant?'

'I'm here.' It was John Henio. 'What is it?'

'Well, it's Stevie –'

'What about him?'

'He got another call. About you, Lieutenant.'

'Is he there?'

'No – that's it. He just took off.'

Tom Katon paid for the gas. He pulled out of the gas station not waiting for change.

'Lieutenant?'

'Could it be that he just went home?'

'Well –'

'Did he say anything?'

'No, Lieutenant. He was just kinda staring and then he took off.'

Tom Katon turned the wheel. 'Okay. I'll deal with it. You let me know if he calls, okay?'

'Okay.'

He replaced the receiver. He was only a block now from Stevie Nez's place. He turned on Second Street and pulled up. The house, a low scruffy-looking building, one of a line, showed no sign of life. The curtains were drawn and there were no cars in the driveway. He switched off the engine and crossed the road. He banged on the door.

'Stevie? You in there?'

He put his ear to the door. Sounds. Someone moving about.

'Lucy? That you?'

The curtains round back were drawn too. He tried the kitchen door. It was open. He eased himself in, aware of the weight of the gun on his hip. The kitchen door giving onto the hall was open. He shouldered the frame and peered round. Nothing.

Then something. A noise. From the lounge.

'Lucy?'

The lounge was empty, the phone upturned on the floor. Tom Katon stepped forward. 'Lucy? Are you there?' he said. Then, before his eye caught it, he sensed movement behind and he turned, but too slow, as outside in the street a garbage bin tumbled and a cat raced away through the shadows.

34

THE OLD NAVAJO TRAILS MOTEL and the store beside it sat crouching by the roadside hopeless and windblown as Stevie Nez approached. He pulled up across the road and sat awhile watching. A lighted Coke sign in the store's scrubby window was the only sign of life. He cut the engine, waiting, listening. The Motel had a brutal stubborn look about it: it seemed carved from the bitter browns of the earth and immovable, a place long since abandoned and forgotten. He opened the door and stepped out. The heat was intense, quivering. Sweat streaked his back. He wiped his palms on his shirt.

All the way since Mexican Water he'd thought about turning back. He'd thought about just pulling off, just forgetting about Frankie Platero and turning back to Shiprock. He'd thought about Lucy (she'd be hopeless in the lounge now, sinking in the love of the children she'd never have and needing him) and he'd really thought he'd turn, but the wheel had stayed straight as if beyond his control. Instead he'd stared at the road, excluding all else, watching himself as if watching from above, knowing he was watching a choice being made.

He crossed the road to the store and pulled on the screen door. The store was long since deserted, the shelves empty. He moved through the aisles to the backroom. The backroom was dark. He flicked the light. Nothing. Boxes. Sagging shelves. A few cans. The buzzing of flies around a putrid bone. He moved back through the store and out.

It's me, Stevie, it's me. If not this then something else. He'd seen it coming like a train around a track. *Do you love me, Stevie Nez?* He'd said yes, not knowing what it meant. Did love mean more than sentiment? More than just the fear of alternatives? Of maybe nothing? More than the fear of no kids, no point? He'd said yes carelessly, as if he'd been saying yes to coffee or a movie, all the time knowing he should be saying I don't know or Maybe and knowing then in the moment of his doubt it wasn't enough and wouldn't last, and knowing then that something would find him out.

He moved down the verandah, around the corner and across the courtyard. The concrete of the courtyard, once flat and white-lined for visitors' cars, was buckled now and split in the heat. He tried the first door. Locked. And the next. He cupped his hands to the window but could see nothing through the grimy glass. He moved along, trying each door. All were locked but one. This, the last, opened inward. He eased back the door and stepped in. 'Hello?' he said, aware of the noise of his boots on bare boards. It was dark in the room, the air thick. He pulled back the curtain and scanned the room. A chair, a table, a narrow dipping unmade bed. Beside the bed, one laceless shoe. Beneath the bed, a rag, a shirt maybe. He touched the bedclothes. Cold. He crossed the room to the bathroom. Standing to one side, he tapped on the bathroom door. 'Frankie? You in there?' Nothing. He twisted the handle. The door opened in. Still nothing. A chipped sink stained brown from a once-dripping tap, a toilet backing up with sewage. Breathing through his mouth he reached up and opened the high narrow window. He stood a moment, breathing the clear air. He made his way back outside.

Once fenced, the yard out back was bled back now into scrub, tufts of thick desert grass reclaiming that which for a while had been denied them. In the shade at the back of the store five tires stood neatly, incongruously stacked. Here and there broken glass lay scattered like seed.

He crossed the scrub and checked the old shed. The air inside was thick with the smell of dogs, the straw at his feet matted. Here and there were piles of drying faeces. He covered his nose and mouth with his sleeve and stepped back outside. He stood still, looking for movement, waiting. Nothing. Just the breeze brushing the thick grass and sending an aerial clicking slowly around on a pole.

*

126

He listened to the radio as he drove back to town, trying not to think about Frankie Platero or Lucy alone in the house, trying just to think about calm safe things, but for all his trying it wouldn't do: all he could think about was how things just weren't working and how maybe he could just turn around and keep going. But he didn't: he drove on, dreading his arrival more with every mile, watching the towns pass by him until something made him slow and he pulled off at Walden. He cut the engine and stepped out. He crossed the road to a bar.

The first went down easy, then the second, third. In a while his head stopped its pounding. He felt his limbs growing heavy as a bitter warmth rose up in him. Lucy, Lucy. He listened, mind drifting, to the sounds of the jukebox.

She is lying on her front on the campus grass, turning the pages of a book. She looks up as he passes by, as if drawn by his looking. 'Hey,' she says.

'Hey.'

She smiles, holds up the book. Hemingway. *The Garden of Eden*. 'Don't you just hate this?' she says. 'All this hair-cutting? All this dryness?'

He says nothing, wanting to but panicking.

'Well?'

'I guess,' he says at last, fumbling, flushing, ashamed half of his fumbling and half of the lie.

She cocks her head and it strikes him (like a thunderbolt, he'll write later in his diary) that this is his chance and he'd better shape up —

'Are you alright?' She is frowning now, watching him, disappointment, boredom, already gathering, and he tries to think but all he can think is this is my chance and I'd better shape up —

'Hey, fella.'

He looked up from his glass. His head was thick with drinking.

'You okay, fella?'

'I'm okay,' he said.

'You look bad, man.'

'I said I'm okay. Okay?'

The barman shrugged and walked away.

Stevie sat awhile half-listening to the jukebox, then he drained his glass and left the bar. He pulled out of the parking lot, hands gripping tight to the wheel, his head full of thoughts he couldn't quite isolate. He was sweating. It was the whiskey. He rubbed his face with his hand. *It's me, Stevie, it's me.* He drove on staring hard at the road, through Crest, through Mexican Water, dreading his arrival more with every mile and what it would ask of him.

35

JIMMY CHAI WOKE from his dreams of flying and stared in the gloom at the airplane's curved insides. The air was thick with sleep and breathing. He closed his eyes and tried to recover his dream but his dream would not be recovered: it had blinked away in the moment of waking and was gone. He pushed himself up. His neck was stiff from the manner of his lying, his mouth dry. He crawled up the cockpit and took a mouthful of water from his bottle. The water was warm. He spat it out through the pilot's glassless window, heard it slap on the hard ground below. He rested his arms on the rim of the window and let his mind wander where it pleased.

He was daydreaming still (flying a P58 Mustang over occupied France) when the scuttling of a prairie-dog on the ground below roused him. He squinted in the sun, watching the prairie-dog burrowing a hole then abandoning it for another. It paused a moment, sniffing at a patch of dark engine oil, then scuttled on, around the edge of the sheep pen. Jimmy Chai watched it until it was gone from sight. He yawned, his eyes drifting back then to the engine oil and the tracks in the dirt. He thought about the guy with the pick-up and wondered where he'd be by now. On the road somewhere, he imagined, windows wound down, heading east on I-40 (he'd be over the line by now, speeding his way through New Mexico to Texas) or maybe west to California and the coast. He closed his eyes. In his mind he saw him turning up the radio, heard the music whipping out and away across the fast-moving back-sliding desert, saw the pick-up, smaller now and smaller, heading up through the heat haze and over the rise, rippling, indistinct, going, gone.

When he opened his eyes the sun was lower, the shadows

longer. He looked at his watch: an hour had passed. *Another hour of my life*, he thought gloomily. He rubbed his eyes and sat for a while, aware of nothing more concrete than the ticking away of seconds on his watch. He'd worked it out once: how many seconds he'd spent sitting in the workshop or out on the stall staring down the sun, his mouth filled with dust, and though he couldn't remember the total now it was somewhere in the millions – several years' worth of seconds spent so carelessly that now he couldn't even remember how he'd spent them. They'd just slipped by unnoticed – seconds making minutes and minutes making hours and so on – until here he was nearly nineteen years old and still he'd only ever been as far from the Pueblo as Albuquerque, and then only on errands and only as far as the Indian Depot on Mission Street. Not that he hadn't thought about going further – just spinning the wheel of the family pick-up and heading off to some place like Chicago or New York and getting a job maybe in a bar or in a factory (there'd be flying lessons to pay for and air-time isn't cheap) – but thinking so far is all he'd ever done, and sometimes he thought that's all he'd ever do and that he'd still be here in the Pueblo in twenty years' time looking back at himself as he is now and wondering where all the seconds and hours and months had gone and why in heaven's name he hadn't just spun the wheel and headed off to Chicago or New York or someplace and got a job in a bar or a factory –

His watch buzzed the hour, unremarked. He sat still, mind disengaged, eyes tracing the progress of a car along the highway. It was the family pick-up, his brothers finished for the day. It slowed, turning onto the Pueblo road, windows glinting in the sun, raising dust at its wheels, and disappeared behind the first of the low sand-colored buildings. In his mind's eye Jimmy Chai could see it pulling up across the road from the house as it always did, then reversing and parking in the shade beside the store. In his mind's eye he could see his brothers crossing the street laughing and joking and disappearing inside, heading for the backroom, the ice-box, the shower. He could see it all just as it had always been. Just as it always would be.

It was after six when he eased himself down from the plane and made his way home through the Pueblo's dusty streets. He didn't speak to Horace Pico when Horace Pico spoke to him. He felt too hollow for talking. Instead he just walked on scuffing his sneakers in the dust, his thoughts sitting heavy on his life like stones.

The front room was empty. He turned on the TV. Oprah Winfrey was talking to a studio full of women, each of whom had red hair. He watched for a while then let his mind drift. There were voices in the backroom: his brothers, his mother, all talking at once. *It can't be true*, he heard his mother say. He turned up the sound and stared at the screen. Oprah Winfrey was crossing the studio, changing her microphone hand to hand. She stopped suddenly and turned to the camera. All behind her went dark. Jimmy Chai frowned. *Do it now*, she said, whispering only to him. He shifted in his seat, uncomfortable suddenly in her gaze. *Turn the key and keep driving*. Now? he said soundlessly. Oprah Winfrey was nodding. His heart was pounding. He stared at the screen, but as suddenly as she'd come Oprah Winfrey was gone. In her place was a man selling shoes.

When she saw the pick-up rising on the road through the haze, Marla Thomson knew at once it was Perry. She touched her hair, straightening it as best she could. She looked a fright, she knew: for a day and a half she'd been scrabbling over ditches and fields of water-melon, scratching her clothes on the spikes of spiteful cacti. For a day and a half her hopes had been fading, but now she knew everything would be alright. She flattened her dress and hitched up a smile and was smiling still when the pick-up pulled up alongside. She cupped her hands and peered through the glass. 'Perry?' she said. The smile froze on her lips. The driver was a large man, red-faced, round-bellied, a baseball cap tipped back on his head that said *USS Arizona*.

'Nope,' said the man. 'Name's Henry.' He was smiling, displaying a set of uneven teeth. 'What you doing out here, darlin'?'

Marla stepped back.

The man leaned over. 'Hey lady – you want a ride or not?'

Marla shook her head.

'You sure now?'

She said she was sure. The man shrugged. He ground his gear-shift and drove away.

Marla watched the pick-up until it dipped over the rise and was gone. She rubbed her eyes. For a day and a half her hopes had been fading; suddenly now they were all but gone. She stood, staring down at the dust on her shoes, aware of her spirit sinking down through her limbs and into the darkness of the earth.

36

MAYBE IT WAS just deceiving distance, but as hard as he tried (and he was trying hard, despite the best efforts of the whiskey to confuse him) Stevie Nez couldn't recall that change-your-life moment when it had all got so damn serious. It all just seemed to have happened: one minute they were dating – movies at the Miramax, a shared table in the library, sitting out beneath the stars on her mother's back step – and the next here they were – same bed, same life, same future. It was as if – looking back now – a coin had been flipped without his seeing, his life decided by sleight of hand, and suddenly now as he drove along it all made him angry, unreasonably angry – he'd been cheated – and he slammed the wheel and the patrol car swerved, over and back, into and out of the path of a late-model Chevy. The Chevy flashed by, horn wailing. Stevie straightened the car, gripping the wheel. Jesus Christ. He drew a hand across his brow. He was sweating hard.

He slowed the car and pulled over. He drew deep breaths for calm. Just tell her. Simple. Just say it straight, no fuss. *This isn't what I meant, Lucy*. It sounded so easy though he knew it wasn't. Especially now. *It's me, Stevie, it's me*. She'd be staring at him, disbelieving, and he'd start feeling guilty like he'd been caught red-handed strangling a cat and he'd feel himself crumbling, giving in, and he'd turn the thing around and they'd end up eating pizza and making arrangements for next week, next month, next year. Then later he'd lie in bed staring at the ceiling, cursing himself for his lack of resolve, but in time he would sleep and in the morning as usual he'd get up and everything would go on until the next time came around, but every time it would get harder as the time passed by and sooner or later he'd just give up and start to tell himself (and start to believe it) that he'd got what he'd wanted all along and wasn't everything wonderful the way it had turned out?

A car sped by, spitting stones, rousing him. He rubbed his eyes. The whiskey lay heavy on his stomach. This time, he thought. He said it out loud. The words sounded fake, but the less so the more he said them. This time, this time, this time. He nodded – to himself, to any passing witness. It was now or never. He started the car and drove off, anxious to begin before resolve slipped away.

He first saw the ambulance on the outskirts of Shiprock. It was turning left, siren wailing, heading the wrong way down Teals Street. He watched it go, heard the siren fade. He drove on, stopping at the Santa Clara Pharmacy. Here he bought some antacid tablets for his stomach and a packet of mints.

He turned left at BigaBite, up past the station. The lot in front of the station was empty, all the squad cars gone. He switched on the radio, but then switched it off. He paused at the lights. He rapped his fingers on the wheel.

He heard the ambulance again three blocks away from home. It grew louder as he neared Second Street. He turned the corner, aware suddenly of the beating of his heart.

They were carrying the body on a stretcher – a medic either end, another holding a drip. He sat for a moment staring, unable to move, but then he was moving, opening the car door and running down the street, his feet slapping hard on the hard ground, his breath coming short, the flesh pulled back from his teeth like he was a madman, grinning and howling –

A hand gripped his arm.

'Hey, Stevie –'

He tugged but there were other arms and he couldn't break free, and all he could see were the doors of the ambulance closing tight and all he could hear were the voices all around him screeching death beneath the vast bleached burning sky.

37

UNSEEN WITHIN THE darkness of the disused water-butt that stood for the purpose of advertisement outside the Santo Doringo store, Jubal Early eased off his socks. His socks were sodden and were starting to sting, thanks to the unwelcome attentions of a dog. He squeezed the socks as well as he was able (occupied water-butts are not long on elbow room and he had to drop his head between his knees), then, that done, he replaced them and resumed his vigil.

In the nearly two days that had elapsed since he'd doubled up his body under cover of night and squeezed it into the butt, Jubal Early had observed much of the ways of the Pueblo. Through eye-holes carved with the aid of a penknife, he'd seen much that was singular but more, alas, that was merely ordinary. Of the singular, he'd watched, intrigued, as an old blind man, thinking himself unobserved, had paused not three feet from him and, with an accuracy of eye normally associated with the seeing, stooped to pick up a dime from the dust. Smiling, the blind man had slipped the dime into his pocket; in the butt Jubal Early had frowned. He'd frowned also (and was frowning still, his eyes stuck like limpets to the house across the track) at the appearance of the dog, for he knew the attraction of a barrel to a dog and also the size of the canine bladder and its consequent short-comings.

The door across the way opened. From within emerged a large stout Indian woman who seemed in quite a state. On her arms, supporting her, were two young men whom Jubal Early guessed were her sons. They crossed the street towards him, then stopped abruptly. The woman, who was crying, looked from one son to the other. She said something. Jubal Early turned his ear to the eye-hole. Gone, she was saying, the pick-up's gone, then something about someone called Tom and a shooting. She was crying hard now. Jubal Early turned his eye to the hole, just in time to witness the woman's collapse, and her sons helping her onto the step. One of the sons – a tall angular dark-skinned Indian – left them then returned a minute later at the wheel of an old beat-up Lincoln. The mother, supported by the other son, got into the car and the car drove away.

A minute passed.

Slowly, inch by inch, Jubal Early pushed on the top of the butt and peered out. He scanned the road: all clear. Since dawn he'd sensed there was something about to happen, and now it had. With the stealth of a burglar he eased himself out of the butt and, stooping low to avoid detection, crept across the road and into the shadows. Since dawn there'd been something in the air (notwithstanding the odours in the butt) – a vibration, a throbbing in the air like the throbbing in the earth in the moments before an avalanche. In the darkness he'd scribbled notes in the pages of his notebook. *Well*, he'd written, and, *Hang Up The Phone*, and, *I'd Be Sitting On The Edge Of My Seat If I Had A Seat To Sit On.*

He moved around the side of the house and peered in the first window. Nothing: just a child sitting still, cuddled up with a teddy bear. He crept to the next window, finding here what some strange extra sense had told him he'd find. He cupped his hands to the glass. The old man was lying on his back on a bed asleep. Jubal Early watched his chest rise and fall. The old man turned; Jubal Early dinked away, feeling as he did so a sharp spear of hunger. He turned from the window and looked all about him. For nearly two days he'd eaten nothing but beetles, grinding them up in his teeth, screwing his face up at the bitter taste. He checked the old man, then crept across the yard to a line of trash-cans. The first was empty. From the second he withdrew a flesh-covered bone and a segment of half-eaten water-melon. He re-crossed the yard and laid the bone and the melon with care on the window-sill. As a child there'd been trouble if he'd eaten without prayer, so as ever he did he closed his eyes. Dear God, he whispered, though as ever then he could think of nothing else to say. He opened his eyes. The old man was on his side now, head buried deep in his pillow. Jubal Early stood a moment, just listening, watching. Then, having brushed away the flies that had gathered on his supper, he lifted the bone and began to eat.

38

THE UNIVERSITY OF New Mexico Medical Center at Farmington was glowing pink in the evening light when Wanda Chai and her sons turned in off the highway. They'd driven the distance from the Pueblo in silence, each lost in their own thoughts, and were silent still as Virgil Chai manoeuvered the old Lincoln into a parking space. He switched off the engine. The engine objected but then was quiet. 'Well,' he said. He looked at his brother. His brother shrugged. Between them, their mother was staring down at her knees, her face as still as the face of a corpse.

'Mama?' said Willie. 'Are you okay?'

Wanda Chai nodded. *If only*, she thought.

'Come on,' said Virgil. He opened the door. The day was cooling, shadows lengthening. He took his mother's hand and eased her out of the car.

'Virgil?' she said.

'Yes, Mama?'

'You'll go find Jimmy, won't you, Virgil?'

'Yes, Mama.'

'He's probably gone off and got lost, or maybe he's visiting with someone,' she said, though they all knew neither was likely: Jimmy knew the roads too well and he had no friends to speak of.

'Come on,' said Virgil. He gripped his mother's arm. Despite her weight, her bones seemed as tiny and fragile as a child's. 'Tom'll be wanting to see you.'

'Virgil's right, Mama,' said Willie. 'You can't keep the cops waiting, can you?'

Oh Tom, thought Wanda.

'Mama?'

'I'm coming,' she said. She sighed then straightened her coat. She let herself be led through the lines of darkening cars.

An eighth of an inch further over to the right and the bullet that had entered Tom Katon from behind would have struck his heart and killed him. As it was, it avoided all major organs and whistled clean through, lodging finally in a window-frame. A thirty-eight calibre dented badly from its contact with the wood, the bullet now sat in a plastic packet in the pocket of Bruce Lasalu's windcheater. He was turning it over in his fingers (had been for half an hour), gazing out of the window, thinking about a decision just made – was he doing the right thing? – when a tapping on the door broke the silence.

He crossed the room, withdrawing his hand from his pocket. He opened the door a crack. 'Yes?'

Wanda Chai was standing in the corridor flanked by her sons. Her face was pale, her eyes red from crying. She swallowed hard. 'Bruce?' she said softly.

Bruce Lasalu nodded.

'Is he gonna be okay?'

'I reckon.'

Wanda Chai dropped slightly from the news as if from a blow. Her sons held her tight.

Bruce Lasalu opened the door wider. 'Do you want to come in?' he said. 'Do you want to sit down?' Though he'd never really liked Wanda Chai, having always found her brusque and hard-tongued, her sudden infirmity made his heart go out to her. 'He's going to be fine,' he said, 'really.' His hand strayed back to his pocket and the bullet. He turned it around, feeling its smooth edges, its crumpled tip.

Wanda Chai stepped gingerly inside, her eyes flitting around her as if she feared assault. They landed at last on the figure on the bed. She swallowed hard.

'Sit, Mama,' said Virgil. He helped his mother into the chair by the bedside. She was staring at Tom Katon's pale face, his eyes ringed with shadow.

'Mama?'

139

She gripped the chair's arms. 'Oh, God,' she said. She was blinking hard, staring at the body. 'What have they done to you? What have they done to you?'

'Take it easy, Mama.'

And then she was crying, the tears rolling hard down her face.

'Mama?' said Virgil. He stepped forward to comfort her but she waved him away. He stood a moment, trying to think of the right words to say, but they wouldn't come. In a while he followed Willie and Bruce Lasalu from the room.

Stevie Nez was in the cafeteria when Bruce Lasalu found him. Bruce Lasalu bought a coffee and a doughnut and sat down beside him. 'Hey,' he said, 'you okay?'

Stevie Nez was staring down at an empty plastic cup. She'll be fine, it's just shock, the doctor had said. An hour and you can take her home. That was two hours ago.

'Stevie?'

He looked up.

'What?'

'It wasn't your fault.'

He shrugged. For two hours he'd been thinking: I should have turned back. For two hours he'd been seeing Frankie Platero in the living-room, smiling, raising a gun, firing at Tom Katon.

'Did they pick him up yet?' he said.

Bruce Lasalu was blowing on the top of his coffee. He shook his head. He put down the cup. 'Look, Stevie –' He paused.

'What?'

He shrugged.

'What?'

'Well, are you sure it was Frankie?'

'I heard him.'

'Yeah, I know you heard him. You didn't *see* him though, did you?'

'I heard him.'

'Yeah, I know.'

'What are you saying?'

'I'm saying can you be sure?'

'I'm sure.'

'I mean, okay, Frankie's an asshole —'

'I said I'm sure, okay?'

Bruce Lasalu looked down at his cup.

They sat a while in silence. Behind the counter, a hugely overweight woman was perched on a stool, one hand holding a half-eaten doughnut, the other a beat-up copy of *Weird But True Magazine*. Every few minutes she took a bite of the doughnut and turned a page, licking her lips and sighing.

'Stevie?'

'What?'

'Ah, nothing,' said Bruce Lasalu.

'What?'

He shifted his cup on the table. 'Did you know I'm quitting?'

Stevie looked up. 'What?'

'I'm quitting.'

For a moment Stevie didn't know what to think, then he smiled. 'You ain't quitting.'

'I have.'

'What?'

'I've had enough, Stevie.'

'You ain't serious.'

'I'm serious.'

'Nah,' said Stevie. 'You can't quit. What the hell would you do? You can't hardly do this.'

Bruce Lasalu shrugged. 'I don't need it no more,' he said. 'Frankie, Luke, all that shit.'

'Are you for real?' said Stevie. He couldn't believe it. Bruce Lasalu had been there for ever.

'For real,' said Bruce Lasalu.

'Jesus,' said Stevie. 'Where the hell're you gonna go?'

Bruce Lasalu shrugged. 'Someplace else.'

'Where?'

'I don't know.'

'Jesus.'

The woman behind the counter looked up for a moment then back to her magazine. Across the room the door opened. Lucy stood in the doorway. They'll be in the cafe, the doctor had told her. She was pale-faced, unsteady on her feet, clutching her bag to her chest like a child keeping hold of a doll.

'Stevie?' she said. Her voice was a whisper. She was squinting in the bright lights.

Stevie Nez was looking down at his hands on the table.

'Hey, Stevie,' said Bruce Lasalu.

Stevie Nez pushed himself up. He walked away from the table, stopped, turned around. 'You really quitting?' he said.

Bruce Lasalu nodded. Behind the counter, the woman on the stool took a bite, turned a page.

39

HE UNDRESSED HER in the dark and put her to bed. In a while, thanks to the pills, she was sleeping. He lifted her hands and folded them under the blankets. He sat back and watched her sleeping, the gentle rise and fall of her chest. He let his eyes close but opened them at once when Frankie Platero, smiling, returned. He pushed himself up. He felt sick to his stomach from the whiskey.

He stood in the chaos of the living-room and looked out at the street. Dusk was falling over Shiprock, night coming on. In a yard across the street the black shape of a dog was nosing through the spillings of an upturned trash-can. A light flicked on, a voice rising sharp through the still-warm air. The dog slunk away, merging with the shadows. The light flicked off. Stillness returned.

All the way home he'd been thinking about Bruce Lasalu, about him leaving and never coming back, about how strange things would seem without him. All the way home he'd been thinking *Maybe I could leave too*, though he knew in his heart he couldn't. There was Lucy. Always there was Lucy. From that moment on campus when she'd first laid her eyes on him, she'd had him in her grasp, for always, for ever and ever.

He turned away from the window and stood amongst the debris. For a while the house had been filled with people – strange voices, the snap of pictures, urgent footsteps in the yard – but now it was quiet and seemed emptier than it had ever been. He bent down and picked up a china figurine and set it back on top of the TV. He twisted the TV back into place (it was facing the wall as if standing in disgrace) and restacked the videos on the shelf underneath. He started straightening the pictures on the old chest that her father had brought back from the war, but then gave it up. There suddenly seemed little point.

He wandered back into the bedroom. Lucy was lying on her back now. Her eyes were open.

'Stevie?'

'Go to sleep,' he whispered.

'Stevie?'

'What?'

'Are you okay?'

He sat on the edge of the bed. He stared down at his boots in the gloom.

'Stevie?'

'I'm fine.'

'Are you?'

'Of course.' He turned. 'You know you should be asleep.'

'Stevie?'

'The doctor said you should rest. You've had a shock.'

'Is he okay?'

'Who? The Lieutenant? Yeah, he's okay. Look, try to sleep, okay?'

'Okay.'

Lucy closed her eyes, but then opened them.

'Stevie?'

'What?'

'I was thinking.'

'Oh?'

'About what you said.'

'What did I say?'

'About moving away. Do you remember?'

'I remember.'

'Well?'

'What?'

'Do you still want to?'

'Now?'

'Don't you want to?'

'I can't.'

'Why not?'

144

'Look, go to sleep, will you?'

'Why not, Stevie?'

'I just can't, okay?'

'But why?'

'Well, my job for one thing. I can't just quit.'

'You can. Bruce Lasalu did.'

Stevie looked up. 'So?'

'So can you.'

He looked away. Bruce Lasalu quitting: the notion seemed absurd and made his stomach churn worse.

'I thought you wanted to,' said Lucy.

'I did.'

'Well then.'

'That was before.'

'Before what?'

Stevie shrugged. Tell the truth, he thought, just tell her straight. 'I don't know,' he said.

'Is it me?'

Tell the truth. He said nothing.

Lucy turned her head to the window. Outside it was dark now. 'I see,' she said, her voice barely a whisper.

Stevie opened his mouth to speak, but nothing – neither lies nor the truth – would come.

'Stevie?'

'Look,' he said at last. He felt a hand on his arm.

'You don't mind, do you? About children? I mean you wouldn't leave me just because of that, would you?'

'Of course not.'

'Would you?'

Tell the truth.

'Stevie?'

'I said of course not. Not because of that.'

The hand withdrew. 'I see. But you would because of *something* –'

'What?'

'Leave me. Because of *something*.'

'Like what?'

'I don't know, do I?'

'Go to sleep,' said Stevie. 'You're getting hysterical.'

Lucy was quiet a moment. Then she said, 'Stevie?'

'What?'

'I was thinking.'

'I know. You said.'

'About a baby. We could adopt a baby.'

'What?'

She was up on her elbows suddenly, her face clear and pale, her blonde hair shining like silver.

'We could get one of those babies from Africa –'

'What?'

'Or India if you want, or Egypt. Dan Rather said there's a million of them, or two million, or something. He said they're just crying out for homes –'

'No,' said Stevie. He was staring at his boots. *Tell her*, he thought. *Just say the words.*

'No?'

He looked up. The whiskey was boiling in his stomach. 'That's right. No. Don't you understand?'

'But we could –'

'No!'

'But –'

He pushed himself up. 'I said no – alright?' He was shouting suddenly, the whiskey pumping like blood in his veins. He could feel himself sweating. There was violence in his hands. He raised them but then let them fall. He stood for a moment, his chest heaving, aware of himself as a man without courage, a man sinking fast, a soul in the grip of a smothering undertow, going down and down –

He crossed the room and closed the door hard and was walking away down the hall, pulling the screen door, hearing it banging, then fleeing like a thief into the deep black starless night.

40

IT WAS AFTER midnight when Tom Katon woke. He lay blinking in the light, aware of a pulse in his head. He turned his head. The light was yellow and spewing from a lamp. The lamp was set on a table, the table of cheap construction — pressed wood, lacquer. He squinted in the glare. Beyond the table, indistinct in the gloom, a figure, a woman, large-limbed, dark-skinned, was sitting bent-necked in a chair, snoozing. The sound of her breathing filled the room. Tom Katon watched the rise and fall of her chest. *Wanda*, he thought, the word coming to him with the surprise of an unexpected gift. *Wanda*. He gazed at her broad face — so peaceful in sleep — and was doing so moments later when she stirred.

'Wanda,' he whispered.

Her eyes were open, but blank still with the blur of sleep. She pushed herself up, rubbing her eyes.

'Tom?'

He nodded, reached out a hand.

'Oh, Tom —'

Then sleep again drew over him like a tide. He felt a hand enfold his. He drifted.

When he woke again the room was bright. Wanda was standing at the end of the bed, and there were others: frowning faces, white coats, clipboards, a man with greying hair and a beard. This man broke away from the group and moved around the bed. He lowered his face. His breath smelled of mint.

'Lieutenant? Tom? Can you hear me?'

The man had teeth of extraordinary regularity, and reminded Tom Katon of someone. It came to him who but the thought slipped away.

'Tom?'

He opened his mouth. His mouth was dry, his lips cracked.

'Good,' said the man. The man smiled again, then withdrew. Tom Katon was aware then of the group moving off, away, like a white cloud moving slow across the sky. He licked his lips. His eyes were heavy. They closed again. He slept.

He slept until one, dreaming of the woman in the chair, when a clicking sound woke him. He opened his eyes. The light was less sharp now – just the yellow of the lamp. He held his breath, listening.

Click, click.

The chair was empty. He turned his head. A figure – a man – was standing at the window, gazing out, his back dark against the light. He had one hand by his side, the other in his pocket. His fingers were moving in his pocket: clicking, metal on metal.

Tom Katon shifted his head. The figure turned.

'Lieutenant?'

He blinked.

'How you doing?'

He shrugged his shoulders: so-so. His head felt as heavy as a boulder. He couldn't feel his legs. He looked down at his feet: they seemed distant, disconnected, paralyzed. Panic crossed his brow.

'Legs,' he whispered.

Bruce Lasalu moved nearer, lowered his head.

'What's that, Lieutenant?'

'Am I –' He couldn't find the word.

'You're gonna be fine,' said Bruce Lasalu.

A door opened. There was movement in the room: bodies to and fro. The man with the even teeth loomed over him. A light shone bright, then everything dimmed.

Minutes passed, like hours.

'Tom? Can you hear me?'

He opened his eyes. The man with the teeth was smiling. His lips were moving. 'Your wife's here to see you, Tom,' he was saying.

Tom Katon frowned.

The man's face withdrew. In its place a woman appeared. It was the snoozing woman from the chair.

'Hello, Tom.'

'Wanda?' he said.

'Oh, Tom.'

He felt the touch of her lips on his cheek, her fingers on his arm.

'Wife?' he said, his voice just a whisper.

'Wife,' said Wanda. She kissed him again and he closed his eyes, and his life that for so long had lain dormant blossomed, and tears filled his eyes like crystals of joy.

41

IT WAS TWELVE FIFTY-SIX and Stevie Nez was cruising aimlessly around Shiprock's darkened streets when he saw Charlie Begay standing on the sidewalk outside BigaBite Burgers. He pulled up across the street and cut his engine. A friend of Frankie Platero, Charlie Begay was a no-hope Navajo who'd done time for stealing cars. He was short and squat with no visible neck and while he always looked stupid, tonight he also looked nervous. He was looking up and down the street, every now and then glancing at his watch.

Stevie Nez slid down in his seat. His stomach was growling with the whiskey and other things. He peered through the windshield, watching Charlie Begay but thinking of Lucy. He pictured her lying on the bed crying. He felt a sharp stab of guilt.

It had never been children before. Before it was always something else. Before, in her mind, she'd thought he'd been planning to leave her because she'd gained or lost weight, because he'd met someone else, because she'd failed as a teacher, because a dozen other things. *I hate you*, she'd say, though without conviction, and she'd pummel his chest, her hands like a child's hands, her wrists so delicate he could circle them with ease with his thumb and first finger. In a while of course she'd be calm and the calmness might last for weeks or even months, but always in the end there'd be something, and the cycle would begin again and he'd find himself standing in the yard so angry he'd lash out at the fence-posts with his fists, or be driving in his car through the hopeless lonely streets just wishing he had the courage to just drive and keep driving. But he never did: he always came back. Maybe he always would.

He heard the Firebird before he saw it, the rasp of its engine rising sharp through the night air. He glanced in his mirror. The Firebird was approaching slowly, showing no lights. It pulled up across the street. Charlie Begay bent down, gesticulating with his hands, then, shaking his head, he got into the car. The car took off, ignored a red light, turned right across the bridge and out of town.

Stevie Nez counted slow to twenty then started the car. He flicked on his lights and eased away from the curb. Turning right at the lights he took the bridge across the San Juan river, his headlights flicking on and off the bridge's metal girders. He felt the wheels dip and bunch as he left the bridge. He turned left on Jalla Street and headed west out of town, out towards the dark drumming desert.

To start with and for a while there'd been no sign of trouble. On the contrary. Sitting out back on her mother's step she'd seemed so confident and so bright, so absolutely certain of the future that she'd made him believe in it too: again and again he'd let her describe for him the houses and the cars and the children and the jobs that would constitute their life, and it had all seemed as certain then as the stars. But the brightest stars burn out in time and so in time had the fantasy. In time there'd been letters – the Manager regrets – and a rising tide of gloom in her eyes. There'd been calls from angry shopkeepers demanding immediate settlement of bizarre and spiralling accounts and itemized phone-bills revealing out-of-state calls to complete strangers. Curtains in time had remained unopened, and an end had come swiftly to the nights spent sitting out back on the step. There'd been an end then to talking, and only recently an end to the shouting. Recently, shouting had been replaced by silence, by tears and despair, by dialing tones left hanging like ribbons in a breeze.

And there was the guilt. He couldn't get away from it. As he passed through Mexican Water, through Teec Nos Pos, through Ryan, it was following him as it always did these days, whispering and tugging, drawing him back. Was it his fault? Could he have done – could he do – more? He stared at the darkness, at the shapes of the dark shifting mountains, as doubt dark as treacle poured into his soul. He turned on the radio but music wouldn't fix it. He gripped the wheel and pushed down his foot but speed wouldn't fix it. It gnawed away with the whiskey in his gut, whispering to him that bad things were happening, would happen, and that he'd better watch out or else. He looked in his mirror. The road behind was black. He stared ahead at the backsliding scrub in his lights. The bright eyes of prairie-dogs sat watching him pass. *Diggin' Up Bones*, sang Randy Travis on the radio. He flicked off the radio and gripped the wheel tight. He drove on.

He pulled off the road a quarter mile before the Navajo Trails and flicked off his lights. He wound down the window. The air was sweet with the scent of juniper. There were voices up ahead, muffled by the warm night air. A car door slammed; a light flickered on in the store, then off. Footsteps crunching on shingle. A sudden blast of music. Silence. He sat a while, waiting. He thought, let them get to doing what they've come here to do. He peered at his watch: two a.m. He checked his pistol, fingering the chambers. He was nervous: there was sweat on his back and on the tips of his fingers. He could feel maybe something bad was going to happen. He pushed the feeling away and stepped out of the car.

The road was loose and crunched beneath his boots. He touched his gun. He was sweating bad. Up ahead, as he drew nearer, he could hear dogs howling and scrabbling in their cages. He could hear the metal chinking of chains.

He passed unseen by the broken pumps and stood shoulders back against the store. He edged around, peering in. The store was dark, the window cold to the touch of his cheek. He moved past the window, paused at the corner. The Firebird was standing in the courtyard, ticking in the cooling air. He stood in the shadows, waiting, listening. Nothing. Dogs. The whisper of wind picking up across the desert. The sudden flare of voices from a room across the courtyard. The voices were voices he knew. He pulled out his gun and crept around through the shadows.

The chalet door was closed, a ragged curtain drawn across the window. He put his ear to the door. There were voices, English accents – the brittle voices of a TV. He eased himself back, raised his gun. His hand was shaking.

'Frankie?'

He licked his lips. His mouth was dry.

'You in there, Frankie?'

Footsteps. The TV snapped off.

He leveled the gun.

'That you, Frankie?'

Breathing. He could hear breathing. His heart was racing and then suddenly he was tumbling, stumbling back, as the echo of a shot reached out across the desert then lost itself in the vast still canyons.

42

FROM THE JOURNAL of Jubal Early, the following.

> *See what we see*
> *Know what we know*
> *No sphere of life beyond*
> *land, sea and stars*

He looked up at the stars. The stars above the Pueblo were fading fast, the sky lightening to dawn. He continued:

> *Nothing is a mystery*
> *There is nothing that*
> *cannot be explained*
> *No God*
> *No God!*
> *Mr Sartre was right*

He lifted his pen, waiting for more, but no more came. In a while he closed his notebook and looked at his watch. The sky beyond the mountains was pinking. He drew a hand around his chin, *aide-penser*. For nearly three hours he'd been standing at the old man's window, waiting. He looked again at his watch, again at the sky. The time was moving on and he'd a mission to complete. He cupped his hands and peered through the window. The old man turned. Jubal Early squinted. He snaked a tongue across his thin lips. Nearly time, he thought, nearly time.

43

IT WAS DAYLIGHT already when Bruce Lasalu pulled up at the Navajo Trails. He cut the engine and sat awhile watching. He'd had a hunch Stevie Nez was coming out here: now he was here he was sure. He opened the door and stepped out. He scanned the store and what he could see of the motel. Nothing. No cars.

'Stevie?' he called.

Silence, the whisper of a breeze. He shielded his eyes and studied the desert. The desert was still – no tracks, no rising dust – just the morning rolling like a tide over the land.

Last morning, he thought. Tonight he'd be halfway through Texas, heading for someplace else, Oklahoma maybe, maybe Florida, the Keys. The Keys, he'd heard, were a place to get lost in, and getting lost was right now what appealed. Just sitting in a bar, unbadged, unrecognized. Just drinking and having folks let him be.

A lizard scuttled past at his feet, disappearing in the shade beneath the car. He crossed the road past the broken pumps and moved down the side of the store. What had once been a yard out back was scrub now: old tires, piles of dust-dry garbage, a long low tumble-down shed. He crossed to the shed and pushed on the door. The door swung in, then back. He eased it open. The air inside was thick with heat and the smell of dogs, the sun pouring in through gaps in the wood slats and hanging in shafts of slow-turning dust. He checked the shed. It was empty. He pulled the door to. He made his way back across the scrub towards the motel.

He was halfway across when he first felt the eyes upon him. He stopped, turned. 'Stevie?' he said. Nothing. Empty space. A leaving boy's nerves, he thought. He walked on, past the tires, into the motel's long arching shadow.

Eyes again, burrowing. He turned again. His heart was thumping.

The dogs – six, seven, eight of them, mangy creatures – were sitting in a half-circle watching, seemingly come from nowhere. The nearest one growled, down in its throat like a ventriloquist. Bruce Lasalu picked up a stone and threw it. The dog bent, avoiding the stone, but otherwise didn't move. It just twisted its head, watching. Bruce Lasalu turned away. His hands were sweating; sweat streaked his back. He'd known a pack of dogs once kill a man down in Bisbee and leave him to rot. He walked steady, crossing the scrub; the dogs waited a moment, as if waiting for permission, then followed, keeping a distance, pad, pad, pad on the hard dusty ground. He stopped; so did they. He walked on. Pad, pad, pad. He stopped, paused, turned slow. The dogs sat watching, hard-eyed and cynical, cocking their heads as he slowly drew out his pistol. A crack and they jumped but didn't run. The dog that had growled before growled again. A signal was passed. All eight started moving.

He dropped the lead dog with two shots. It lay twisting on the ground, beating its leg in the dust as if all the life left in it had gathered there. He fired again, the crack echoing out across the desert. The dog howled and was still. He cocked the pistol, aiming, covering the others as they slunk away. They crept into shadows and were gone. He lowered the pistol. Jesus Christ. His heart was thudding. He told himself to calm down.

His eye caught the body when he turned the corner. It was lying face down in the doorway of the motel's furthest room. He froze. There was blood dark as oil on the wooden verandah and a hole in the center of the door about the size of a fist. For a moment he couldn't move: his legs were stuck solid. It was Stevie: he knew it. He swallowed hard. And then he was running, crossing the courtyard, aware of the cool of the breeze on his face, the sound of his boots in the dirt.

44

IT WAS THE policy of Thomas J. Jackson, owner and Editor-in-Chief of *Weird But True Magazine*, to encourage in all his employees a degree of singlemindedness which in the outside world might be deemed excessive. In the pursuit of a story, agents in the field (for such were they known) were encouraged to employ any means necessary (up to and including those rather less than legal), for, in the mind of Thomas J. Jackson, there was nothing — not honor, not the law — that wasn't worth sacrificing in the service of truth.

So it was with this in mind that Jubal Early, on that clear summer morning, was able to embark on his chosen course of action without fear of the censure of conscience. After all, was kidnapping so wrong when mankind had so much to gain? No, he reasoned, as, now putty-free thanks to the blade of his penknife, the glass in the frame of the old man's window came away in his hands. This he set with care on the ground, beside the remnants of his supper. He paused for a moment, looking this way and that. The coast was clear. He hitched up his coat. He eased himself into the room.

The room was gloomy despite the daylight, the air warm and thick like the air in an attic. Jubal Early made his way across the room. The old man stirred; he froze. He could hear his heart beating, see the worry of dreams on the old man's face. The old man opened his mouth as if to speak, then turned, pushing his feet out from under the covers, sleeping on. His feet were white and bony, skin surprisingly smooth. As was his nature, Jubal Early counted the old man's toes. There were ten.

The old man was light to lift. It was like lifting a small roll of carpet. Jubal Early moved with ease to the window, paused, retraced his steps. From the upturned box beside the bed that stood in for a table, he removed a small brown bottle of pills. *Do not drive or consume alcohol*, he read. He slipped the bottle into his pocket and was glad to have done so, for the importance of pills, in the view of Jubal Early, could scarcely be overestimated.

It was awkward getting back through the window but he managed it. As before, he checked the coast. As before it was clear. Then, in order to achieve greater comfort for both, he re-arranged his arms around the old man's knees and shoulders, then set off along his pre-ordained route.

Of course it was a stop-and-start business. Although it was still early, the Pueblo was starting to wake and he had to pause now and then on a corner or in the shadows in order that those residents who were up and going about their business should do so without spying him and remarking in strong terms on his curious burden. At every stop he took the chance to examine the old man's face for signs of wakefulness, but none – thanks of course to the pills – was revealed.

A meticulous planner, Jubal Early had planned his life thus far with the precision of a person to whom precision is a God, and never more so than now. Now, as he zig-zagged the streets of the Pueblo, dipping into shadow and out into light, he knew exactly where he was going. From his water-butt outside the store he'd often had little else to do but examine the activities of Horace Pico, neighbor of the Chais, and in particular those of his activities that had to do with that man's beat-up Thunderbird. From his position of gloom, Jubal early had noted with interest what Horace Pico, on returning from work every day, did with his Thunderbird's keys, which was nothing. Every evening they just sat there dangling in the ignition, just asking for someone to twist them. Well, that someone would be Jubal Early: he'd known this – been planning it – even while his socks had been stinging with piss. *The means of escape mean the means of survival*: such was Thomas J. Jackson's most favored phrase, a phrase well learnt by Jubal Early. Jubal Early always knew how to escape.

The shadow was deep in the alley beside the store. He paused with his burden, watching. Across the dusty street, the Thunderbird was sitting asleep and unattended as he'd known it would be. He edged out his thin head and peered right. Nothing. He swiveled, peering left. A woman was beating dust from a bright-colored rug. He pulled back his head and waited. For distraction, he thought for a moment of the curious consistancy of the soup he'd been forced to drink in school, then, time having passed, he risked another look. The woman was gone, only the dust remained. He hitched up his burden. He licked his thin lips. He walked with audacious calm across the street.

The car started first time, as he'd known it would. He pushed in a button and ground the shift to drive. With a glance at the old man (the old man was slumped on the front seat beside him, snoozing), he eased off the handbrake and pushed down his foot. The Thunderbird rumbled as its tires covered ground. Jubal Early gripped the wheel and stared hard at the dirt road ahead. He touched the gas; the Thunderbird lurched. Beside him, Ethan Pierce snoozed on.

45

IT WAS NOW four o'clock in the morning and Stevie Nez felt like sleeping so bad that when he pulled up at the lights outside BigaBite Burgers after driving all the way from the Navajo Trails he nearly did just that. His hands fell away from the wheel and his head dropped and if it hadn't been for Slicker Skeety blasting the horn of his sixteen-wheeler he'd have slipped so deep into such a deep sleep that he'd probably have slept for a week. But as it was the blast sat him upright (made him wonder for a moment where he was) and he eased down his foot and pulled away.

He turned left on Dayle and stopped the car. He rubbed his eyes and checked himself in the mirror. He looked real bad and he wasn't surprised. He felt real bad. He felt as if he'd been driving for hours, which he had, and like he'd drunk too much whiskey, which he also had. He squinted at his watch: four seventeen and the town around him was sleeping. He thought about Lucy and then tried not to. He tried not to think about anything.

He woke abruptly to the sound of voices. An hour had passed. He sat himself up. A ways down the street two men were arguing, one shaking his fist, the other shrugging. Stevie Nez drew a hand across his face. In his dreams Frankie Platero had been tumbling backwards again, his mouth fixed open in surprise, his hands clutching at the hole in his chest, trying hopelessly to stem the red flow. In his dreams he'd been shouting, his pistol hot in his hand and his heart thumping and his voice rasping hoarse with the dust and the shouting and all the time he was feeling *Don't This Even Things Up* and even *Don't It Feel Good*, and then he was watching Charlie Begay and the others taking off and emptying his pistol into the dust at their wheels and enjoying it and hearing laughing and a voice howling like a hungry coyote and realizing it was *his* laughing, *his* voice –

The men up ahead were gone now. He sat still and stared out at the now-light sky. It was blue bleeding to white and cloudless, the early sun throwing shadows on the sidewalks and spearing the gaps between curtains. He started the car and let it run awhile, but then switched it off. He watched a car approaching, draw level, pass by. He listened to its engine until it was gone.

What was troubling him most was he couldn't say for sure he'd not meant to do it. He'd meant to do something alright, and maybe shooting Frankie Platero had been it. He couldn't be sure any more. All he could remember was feeling trapped and storming out of the house with a rage inside him and feeling sure as he drove that something bad was going to happen. Well something bad had happened and now he felt sick. He'd been out of control and it was scary. He touched his gun, watched his fingers curl their way around the handle. A few hours ago, that gun, those fingers had taken a man's life as easily as picking fruit from a bowl: just a finger squeezing and the crack of a bullet racing out of a chamber, then a man howling unseen the other side of a door.

He jumped at a knock on his window.

'Are you okay?'

It was an old man peering in. Stevie Nez nodded.

'You sure?'

'Sure,' he said. He watched the old man walk away, his body shimmering in the heat off the road.

Second Street was quiet when he pulled up. He got out and crossed the bare lawn to the door. He paused a moment, his key in the lock. Last chance for turning back was now. He stood still, listening, waiting for some kind of direction. When none came – just silence – he twisted the key and opened the door.

The curtains were still drawn, the air in the house thick and stale. He moved slowly through the shadows to the bedroom.

Lucy was sleeping as peaceful as a child, her troubles obscured by dreaming. He took off his jacket and lay down beside her. He closed his eyes. He felt so tired. Soon he was sleeping, unaware of the world and especially of Lucy when she woke. She lay for a moment staring up at the ceiling, then slipped soundlessly from the covers and stood beside the bed. Stevie Nez slept on, unaware of her watching him or the strange cool resolve in her eye. As he dreamed of Bruce Lasalu driving out of the Nation and into the world she thought of Tom Katon and how she'd never meant him harm, how she'd just meant to teach Stevie a lesson, how, when she'd stepped from the shadows and moved up behind him she'd seen just the figure of a man in a uniform, heard the blast of the pistol in her hand, seen the wrong man fall down. She stared hard at Stevie Nez, watched him turn in his sleep. She smiled. He'd come home as she'd always known he would, and she knew in that moment, for the first and surest time, that despite what was coming (and something *was* coming, she knew it — questions and consequences — but she didn't care) he'd never leave her now, never ever, and that now and forever they'd always be together, forever and ever, amen.

Five

46

HAD HE BEEN someone else he'd have maybe just driven by, but Jimmy Chai was Jimmy Chai and he couldn't. Not that he didn't want to — not that he didn't try to just keep going, to just mind his own business, to just think about Tucson and the 57th Tactical Air Wing and pulling back on the stick and rising high through the clouds like a dolphin rises high through the surf — he tried but he just couldn't do it. His heart wasn't in it. He had to slow the pick-up and he had to back up. He had to get out and take a look.

He knelt down in the dirt on the edge of the highway.

'Hey, you okay?' he said. (Sure, like everyone you find lying face-down by the roadside in the middle of the desert's okay. He felt stupid.) He leaned forward and tried for a pulse. It was low but steady. He eased the body over. It was a woman — forty, maybe fifty. Her skin was raw and dusty from the road and the sun, her shirt ripped probably from the way she'd fallen, the curve of her breast pure white. Jimmy Chai looked around him. She'd have to have been walking for miles — days maybe — unless she'd been hitching, unless somebody'd dumped her. He went back to the pick-up and opened the passenger door. He pulled out his stuff and slung it in the back. He paused. I could just keep going, he thought, though he knew he wouldn't: the thought was just a thought and could never be more. He sighed. Jimmy Chai was cursed with strong conscience. He moved back around the truck and picked up the body.

'You're what?'
  'I'm kidnapping you.'
  'Kidnapping?'

'I believe so.'

Despite the obvious movement of the car for a moment Ethan Pierce thought: I'm dreaming. He closed his eyes tight, counted five, opened them. He looked down at his hands. Jesus Christ. He wasn't dreaming. His hands *were* tied together with string, his ankles too. Hardly daring to, he looked at the driver. The driver was a long thin weedy sort of man, narrow nose, sunken cheeks — the sort of individual who looks like he'll drop if he doesn't get a square meal and fast. He had bony hands — bones wrapped in paper — and what with the extra tight way they were gripping the wheel, combined with the fluttering of his feet from pedal to pedal as if he couldn't decide which one to use next, Ethan Pierce was thinking, *Jesus H. Christ, if he ain't planning to kill me then his driving sure is*, and if he'd had just the tiniest piece of religious feeling left in him then he'd have been down on his knees (if it hadn't been for the string) praying to the Lord to deliver him if He could and preferably right now. But he didn't and he couldn't so instead he settled on silence, trying to think.

'I ain't never done this before,' said the driver. His voice was light, as if he were admitting that he'd never before fixed a whiskey and soda. He frowned. 'Kidnapping, I mean, not driving. Driving I done lots o' times. Over two times in fact.'

Ethan Pierce thought, *Oh Jesus*. In a sudden flash vision he saw himself lying lifeless on the side of the road, his corpse oozing blood from a number of holes. He cleared his throat. Maybe silence was dangerous. He'd read once how silence can drive a person nuts. 'Look,' he started. His throat was dry as dust. He paused, uncertain. What should he say? He'd read also some place that a person in a hostage situation should at all times act tough and above all never ever plead for mercy. He drew a silent breath. 'I'm warning you,' he said. It was unconvincing, pathetic, and he felt like pleading and he nearly started but instead he pressed on: 'if you don't stop the car right this minute, then —'

He stopped at a shake of the driver's head.

'No, sir, I can't do that. Leastways not yet.'

Not yet! Ethan Pierce could have cried with relief. He swallowed hard, feeling suddenly like celebrating — Not yet! — but then he thought: It's a ruse. Any minute he *will* stop the car and then bingo: brains on the highway, an unwilling son doing duty by a graveside. He tried to pull himself together.

'I mean it,' he said.

'Me too,' said the driver.

'Please?' It just slipped out. Ethan clenched all his muscles, ready for the blast.

But the driver said nothing. He just changed his mind some about the pedals and went on gripping the wheel. The car lurched and growled. Ethan Pierce closed his eyes. Silence, he decided, was maybe best after all.

47

SINCE THE DEATH of his father, the life of Vernon E. Pierce, proprietor of Vern's Bar and Grill in the city of Boulder City in the state of Nevada, had been going on along just about the same as it had always gone along in all but one respect. It wasn't that he liked his father any more than he had done over the last twenty-odd years, it was more what with him being dead and all he just couldn't seem to raise the energy to hate him any more: a chapter had finally been closed. Besides, he had other things to think about – the restaurant, Clare, the kids, state tax and income tax (he owed, at least they claimed he owed, at any rate he was getting himself worked up enough to fight them), not to mention all manner of other things that were getting piled high on the little man these days when all the little man was trying to do was provide for his family and not go crazy in the process, when all he was trying to do was live the American way like he saw (or more to the point his kids saw) on his TV every morning. Specially now, with the dam's anniversary coming up, he was flat out from five a.m. or thereabouts until way past midnight buying produce, sorting out rosters (and other staff problems you wouldn't believe), cooking, cleaning up, cashing up, and on top of that as always there were the kids to see to (Janice was six and needed picking up from school and Clare had her classes twice a week and couldn't go those days), and on and on and on. There was certainly no time for hating, what with hating taking time to do properly, so days these days went by without Vern thinking once of his father. His father was slipping – had slipped – from his mind. He had other things to think about. More important things.

Like the anniversary for one thing and the fact that it would mean more business for the town (there was a ceremony planned with the Governor and TV and all that went with it), and specifically, in the case of Vern's Bar and Grill, the pressing need for more staff. To this end he'd spent a fortune on a half-page ad in the *Boulder City Clarion*. It was this ad that had brought to him, on that clear summer morning, the vision that was Mrs Miller.

He studied her résumé. He was sitting at his desk in his office off the kitchen. Across the desk, Mrs Miller was smiling.

'Elvis,' she said.

He looked up. 'Excuse me?' When she smiled (she'd been doing nothing else since she'd tapped on his door) Mrs Miller – Vivienne Ann from her résumé – had the look of a woman who'd smiled so hard through so much disappointment that she'd somehow got stuck smiling.

'Elvis,' she repeated. 'Did you see?'

'See?'

She leaned over the desk and ran a finger upside down down the list of her previous employers. 'There,' she said, tapping the page. 'See?'

Cook to Elvis Presley, Vern read. He looked up.

'You were Elvis's cook?'

Vivienne Miller nodded proudly, though honesty brought forth from her the intelligence that she'd been only one of seven. 'One for every day of the week, he had,' she said. 'I was Tuesday. Steaks mostly it was. Even at breakfast. Elvis liked a good steak. Said they reminded him of something.'

'Oh?' said Vern, despite himself. Although he had fifteen more people to see (they were sitting out front coffee-drinking him bankrupt), there was something about this woman that was different.

'Never said what it was though,' she said. 'And I didn't like to ask. He was a very private person, you know, Elvis was. Did you know he hated telephones?'

Vern Pierce shook his head. 'Mrs Miller,' he said.

'Tuesday.'

'Pardon me?'

'Tuesday – that's what people call me. That's what Elvis called me. "Here comes Tuesday", Elvis would say. So that's why people call me Tuesday. You can call me Tuesday too.'

'Right,' said Vern. He pushed himself up. 'Perhaps you could wait outside –'

'Okay.'

Mrs Miller half rose but then sat back down. She looked down at her hands.

'Are you all right?' said Vern. She looked suddenly pale. And then it occurred to him: This woman is starving. I have Elvis Presley's cook in my office and she's starving. He moved around the desk and, looking down at her shoulders, he saw for the first time how thin they were, and also her hands, her wrists. Her wrists were as thin as a child's. 'Look – are you okay?' he said. 'Mrs Miller?'

Mrs Miller nodded.

'Have you eaten?'

'Wednesday,' she said.

'Last Wednesday?'

She nodded. It was Monday.

'Jesus,' said Vern. He touched her shoulder. She flinched. 'Hang on.' He went to the door and called for Clare.

'Mr Pierce?'

There were voices overhead, then footsteps on the stairs. He turned, just in time to see the thin woman crumple, hear the breath leave her body in a faint anguished sigh.

48

WHEN SHE CAME to from her fainting Marla Thomson thought she knew exactly what was happening because of what she'd seen in her dream. In her dream she'd been driving with Perry in a pick-up, bowling through the desert with no time to waste on their way to a date with a preacher. *I do*, she'd been saying, rehearsing, over and over; she was rehearsing still as she drew up from sleep. She stretched her arms, yawning.

'You're awake then,' said Jimmy.

She smiled and turned to feast her eyes on the face of her husband-to-be. The smile froze at once. 'Who are *you?*' she said, alarm rising fast. 'What on earth's going on?'

Jimmy Chai glanced over. The woman was red-faced suddenly and seemed about to explode. It crossed his mind that she might do something crazy — reach for the wheel or something. He gripped the wheel tight. 'I found you,' he said. 'You'd collapsed.'

'Found me? Collapsed?'

'By the side of the highway.' Jimmy glanced across again. 'Are you okay? You look kinda het up.'

I'm dreaming, thought Marla. She closed her eyes tight. Sure enough, there was Perry, dressed for the wedding in a pale grey suit. But then she opened her eyes and Perry was gone. In his place was an Indian in an open-necked shirt.

'Do you want me to stop?' he said. 'Are you going to be ill?'

'I do,' she whispered, a last echo from her dream.

The pick-up screeched to a halt.

'What are you doing?' she shrieked.

'You told me to stop!'

'What?'

'You said you were going to be ill!'

'Ill?'

'Well, are you?'

A shaft of black doubt speared Marla's soul. 'What are you going to do?' she said.

'Do?'

She opened her mouth but decided on silence. To suggest murder or rape might give the man ideas.

'Look,' he said. 'I'm driving along, right? I see a body by the side of the road – your body – right? Maybe I shoulda just left you. Well, I didn't. I'm sorry.'

Marla frowned. For a moment she thought he was going to start crying. She squinted, studying his profile, and realized then that the man she'd seen at first was really just a boy. She relaxed a degree. 'I thought you were Perry,' she said.

The boy said nothing. He was looking straight ahead. So did she. The road up ahead was empty and flat, shimmering in the heat. She thought about Perry as memory returned.

They drove awhile in silence. It was Jimmy who spoke first. 'Do you wanna go to the hospital?' he said. He looked over. Marla was staring down at her hands. 'Did you hear me?' he said.

She shook her head.

'You mean you didn't hear me or you don't want to go to the hospital?'

'I don't want to go to the hospital.'

'Where *do* you want to go?'

She shrugged.

'Where were you going? You must have been going somewhere.'

Marla stretched then curled her fingers. Her fingers were ringless – a spinster's fingers. She shrugged. She looked up. 'Where are *you* going?'

'Tucson.'

'Tucson? Why're you going there?'

'Can't say,' said Jimmy. 'It's private.'

'Private? Why?'

'I said I can't say.'

Marla Thomson looked away, gazing out of the window. In a while she said, 'I was going to Boulder.'

'Boulder? Why?'

'Can't say,' she said. 'It's private.'

49

THEY LAID TUESDAY Miller on the bed in Janice's room and let her sleep. When she woke they fed her chicken soup and listened to her talking. She seemed to need to talk. She told them all about her journey from Memphis, about her jobs along the way, about frying hamburgers in Jonesboro, Arkansas, about packing orthopedic shoes in Tulsa, Oklahoma, about scrubbing floors in Sheridan Lake, Colorado. She told them how Elvis had liked peppers on his steak and how as a girl she'd met the Big Bopper. She talked and they listened, then she slept some more and was sleeping still when the doctor arrived. He sat on the edge of the bed and studied her. He touched her arm with infinite gentleness.

'Mrs Miller?' he whispered. She stirred but didn't wake. He turned to the window where Vern Pierce was standing. 'If you've things to do, Vern,' he said.

Vern Pierce turned away from the window. 'Pardon me?' He'd been watching a Buick turning into a space at the back of the Boulder Best Western. He'd once had a Buick himself, or rather his father had.

'I said if you want to get on –'

'Is she gonna be okay?'

'Sure. She's gonna be fine. She just needs rest. A little gentle feeding.' He frowned. 'You look like you could use some rest yourself.'

Vern shrugged. 'Busy time,' he said. 'The anniversary and all.'

'People gotta eat, huh?'

'People gotta eat.'

The woman stirred. Vern Pierce watched a moment as Doctor Buffet checked her forehead, then he left the room.

Clare was in the restaurant stacking ashtrays on the bar. 'She okay?'

'Yeah, fine,' said Vern. 'Any problems?' He took stock of the room. Although it was still early they were already half-full.

Clare shrugged. 'Too many customers. Not enough help. Same as ever, you know.' She stacked the last ashtray on the pile. 'You get her number?' she said. She was smiling.

'What're you smiling at?'

'You.'

'What did I do?'

There was a crashing of plates in the kitchen. 'Jesus,' said Vern. He went to investigate. When he came back Clare was at the register. She was smiling at a cowboy in a stetson and boots. 'Well?' she said when the cowboy was gone.

'Alice,' said Vern.

'Again?'

He was wiping something red from his shirt.

'How many this time?'

He shrugged.

'We got any left?'

'Excuse me,' said a woman in a bright print dress. The woman was angry and out-of-state. 'I ordered my eggs over easy. Well – ' She held up a plate, displaying its half-eaten contents. 'These eggs may be over but they sure ain't easy –'

'Gotta go,' said Vern, stepping back. He looked back from the kitchen. Clare was still smiling, this time at the woman, and it struck him then, as it struck him several times every day, how beautiful she was and how lucky he was and he took strength from her beauty and his luck, enough and more to face Alice and her plates and whatever else the morning might bring.

It was noon when he made his way up to see Tuesday. He tapped on the door and entered. She was sitting up, sipping a bowl of soup. She looked much brighter.

'How you doing?' he said.

She dabbed her mouth with a napkin and lowered the bowl. 'Oh, Mr Pierce,' she said. Her eyes were suddenly filled with tears.

'Vern, please. Are you okay?'

She nodded. 'Oh, you've all been so kind. I don't know what to say. I'm so sorry –'

'Sorry? For what?'

'For being such a nuisance.'

'Nonsense,' said Vern. He sat on the bed. 'Any friend of Elvis, you know.'

Tuesday smiled. It was a different smile, a sweet smile. For a moment she looked like a child.

'Is there anything you want?'

She shook her head.

'You'll sing out if there is?'

'Okay. Mr Pierce?'

'Vern.'

'Thank you.'

Vern nodded. He stood up. 'There's just one thing,' he said, pausing at the door. 'I'm gonna need a number. Social Security.' He frowned. 'You do want the job, I take it?'

Tuesday's eyes opened wide. 'You mean –'

'Of course, if you don't –'

'Oh I do! I do!'

'Good,' said Vern. 'That's settled then.' He twisted the handle. 'Oh, and one other thing. Marianne – one of the girls – says she's got a spare room. You interested?'

At this Tuesday Miller started crying. She was crying still at the joy of it all as Vern closed the door and made his way down the stairs.

50

FOR NEITHER ETHAN Pierce nor for Jubal Early had the morning so far been going quite as expected. While for Ethan this was a good thing (he'd been expecting death at any moment, but come noon somehow he was still alive), for Jubal Early it most certainly was not. For Jubal Early, the progress he'd expected had not been made; indeed, those bonds between captor and captive which some reading on the subject had led him to expect were still quite conspicuous by their absence. By now (nearly four whole hours had passed since they'd left the Pueblo) he'd expected at the very least a ready exchange of personal details, and to this end – quite redundantly it seemed – he'd worked up a list in his head. Blue, he'd planned to answer if asked his favorite color, and he'd settled on Mama Tee's Oatmeal Muffins as his favorite food. But to no avail. At least so far. So far, apart from the growling of the car on the highway, all there'd been was silence, and silence was no good. Two people cannot bond (and be expected thereafter to reveal their secrets) in silence. It was time for a new tack. Still gripping the wheel he glanced across at the old man. 'Yous hungry?' he said. The old man said nothing. He had his eyes shut as if he were praying. Jubal Early turned away, drove on.

It was nearing one o'clock and his break when Richard Bargello, philosophy major at Arizona State and part-time employee at the Big Belly Diner a mile off the highway three miles shy of Phoenix, looked up from his Sartre at the sound of an incoming car. He peered across the empty diner (it was a slow day, but then every day these days was slow at the Big Belly Diner), out through the grimy windows. The car was an old Thunderbird, beat-up and dusty and seemingly barely under human control.

'Jesus,' he said, watching it come on. The car was crossing the parking lot, heading straight for the diner, when it suddenly slewed, losing speed in a cloud of dust, spun a half-circle and stopped. He turned to the back. 'Hey, Vince,' he said, 'is this place of yours insured?'

Vince Singer stuck his head through the serving-hatch. 'Wassat?'

'I was just wondering if you're insured against, well, everything –'

'What?'

Richard Bargello nodded to the parking lot. 'Accidental demolition by low-flying Thunderbirds, for instance?'

A short-sighted mild-mannered former airplane mechanic who'd always dreamed of owning a diner and now for the life of him couldn't think why, Vince Singer peered out at the car skewed sideways in the empty parking lot. The driver's door was open, a tall thin man in a hat and long coat walking slow through the dust to the door. The closer he got the stranger he looked. He pushed on the door. The door as it opened played the first seven bars of *God Bless America*.

'Can I help you?' said Richard Bargello.

Jubal Early raised his hat in a greeting. Then, catching sight of the face in the hatch, he raised it again. With each raising a small cloud of dust rose and fell. 'Well,' he said looking up at the menu-board, 'I'm looking for food is what I'm looking for.'

'Ah, food,' said Richard Bargello. He nodded. The man quite clearly was another inmate from the County Asylum up in Prescott and, like those before him, needed humoring. He scratched his chin, frowning. 'Let me see now. Food, food – yep, I think we got food. Any particular kind of food, was it?'

'The kind of food that makes a person who ain't inclined to talk talk. Do you have that kind of food?'

Richard Bargello shot a glance at Vince. Once a week on average the Prescott Asylum mislaid a patient; invariably, as if equipped at the gate with a compass and a map, they all sooner or later seemed to turn up at the Big Belly Diner. Last week's arrival was a woman in a smock who'd sat in a corner fellating a spoon until the authorities had turned up and removed her. Richard Bargello scratched his head. 'You mean like conversation food? Chat-snacks? That kind of thing?'

'Yessir.'

'Well, I don't know.' He shrugged. 'But then I'm just the help around here. Big questions like that you'd better address to the boss –'

'What?' said Vince Singer.

'Gentleman here's got a question for you, boss –'

Vince Singer looked miserably at the lunatic, regretting again, as he daily did, the burden of the diner and the dregs of humanity it seemed to attract.

'Sir,' said Jubal Early, turning to the hatch, 'I was just enquiring –' He jumped as the hatch door dropped shut. From behind it in a moment came the sound of crashing pans, the dialling of a number, a voice on the phone.

'Doughnuts? Is that it?'

Jubal Early peered into the large brown bag. Within were a total of seventeen doughnuts, purchased at a cost of one hundred and seventy-six dollars and twenty-one cents. 'I believe so,' he said.

Ethan Pierce shook his head. Despite the seriousness of his circumstances he was starving. 'What the hell'd you get doughnuts for? Couldn't you get nothing else? I hate doughnuts!'

Jubal Early said nothing. He thought it kindest not to mention that the poor soul who'd sold him the doughnuts at such a ridiculous price was quite clearly off his head and in need of understanding not censure. Also, how could he explain that it was through the persuasive qualities of doughnuts (why it had struck him that they had such qualities he didn't know, but it had) that he hoped to gain access to the man's big secret? Best to say nothing, he reasoned. He settled the bag on the bench-seat between them and arranged his feet on the pedals. He glanced over at the old man. 'There's some jelly ones,' he said, but the old man said nothing. Jubal Early touched the gas and the Thunderbird growled. He'd have to think of something else.

*

It came to him on the outskirts of Phoenix. Fear. He veered through the traffic and pulled up on the shoulder.

'Why are we stopping?' said Ethan. From out of nowhere a chisel appeared at his chin. Its metal shaft was cool against his flesh. *Here we go*, he thought, but then he thought, *Here?* The cars on the highway were moving slow: alongside, slipping by, a family – mom, dad, three kids, a dog – were straining to see. 'There's people watching!' said Ethan, his voice suddenly a squeak.

But Jubal Early didn't care. Jubal Early knew about people. He knew that in Memphis in the spring of last year a woman had been raped in a crowded theater and no one had raised the alarm. He knew that people like to see what they know they shouldn't, then like to pretend they haven't. He pushed a little harder with the chisel. 'Tell me,' he hissed, his voice a mean whisper.

'Tell you what?' *Oh God*, thought Ethan, appalled suddenly with the prospect of his blood.

'You know,' said Jubal Early.

'I don't!'

Jubal Early prodded with the chisel, but his heart wasn't in it. As a boy he'd witnessed the death of a bird and from that day on death had been an enemy. He lowered the chisel. 'I'm mean,' he said, trying to compensate, 'and don't you forget it, okay?'

'Okay,' said Ethan. His heart was thumping. From the corner of his eye he saw the man's hands were shaking. Now, he thought, I could jump out and run. But then he remembered the string. How far would he get with his arms and legs tied? He took a deep breath. 'Look,' he said, 'if you tell me what you want –'

Jubal Early was scowling.

'Is it money?'

He was turning the chisel over and over in his lap. 'I'd be obliged,' he said.

'What?'

He turned sharply. There was anger or something in his pale eyes. 'I'd be obliged if you'd let a man think.'

'Sorry,' said Ethan. He looked out at the highway. Up ahead

the traffic was moving faster now. He watched the cars gathering speed, moving on. He felt suddenly so lonesome he thought he might cry. 'It ain't money,' said Jubal Early, but Ethan didn't hear. He was thinking suddenly of his failings — of the foolishness and the pride — that had led him to this point in his life, lost and unmissed. He thought of the care he'd once taken in his work when he'd thought that work was all that mattered, and he thought about Vern and a family cast adrift. He hung his head. There were tears behind his eyes. How could a man be so foolish? How could he have lived so long and have learned so little? He lifted his bound hands and rubbed his eyes. He wished God would strike him down here and now.

But God didn't strike him down. He let His servant live — but more than that, He pulled from the sky the bones of a plan and slipped them with stealth into the old man's head. Ethan blinked twice. He glanced at Jubal Early.

'Okay,' he heard himself saying.

'Pardon me?' said Jubal Early.

'I said okay. I'll tell you.'

Jubal Early narrowed his eyes, the better to detect false manoeuvers. 'You will?' he said.

'On one condition.'

Eyes still narrowed, he raised a skeptical brow. 'Which is?'

'That you take me where I say.'

Jubal Early thought a moment, then reached forward and twisted the Thunderbird's key. The Thunderbird grumbled as if pulled from a deep sleep. 'It's a deal,' he said cannily, for what could he lose?

51

'BUT WHY BOULDER?'

'Why Tucson?'

It was an impasse, a balance of secrets.

'I told you,' said Jimmy Chai. 'It's private. Personal.'

So is planning to leap off a dam and drown, thought Marla, though she didn't say so. Instead she just huffed and looked out at the desert. The desert was empty. It had never seemed emptier. The further south they drove the emptier it became.

They stopped for gas at Oracle. Marla went to buy tapes from the shop. When the pick-up was full, Jimmy went to find her. She was sitting in a booth in the restaurant drinking Coke through a straw. There was a pile of tapes on the table.

'What'd you get?' said Jimmy, sliding in.

Marla shrugged, went on drinking.

The tapes were all country – Steve Wariner, Dwight Yoakam, Vince Gill. The odd one out was a spoken-word tape: *The Great Gatsby* read by Sam Waterston. Jimmy picked it up, turned it around; without leaving off drinking, Marla snatched it back. She turned her head sharply and stared out at the parking lot.

They sat in silence, except for the sound of Coke being drawn through a straw. In a while, Jimmy pushed himself out of the booth.

'You coming?' he said.

Marla let slip the straw from her mouth. 'You going to Boulder?'

'Nope.'

She shrugged and went back to her drinking.

'Please yourself,' said Jimmy. He crossed the room. The door banged behind him.

He drove a mile or so south before something made him stop. He pulled off the highway, switched off the engine.

The truth was being alone made him lonesome. It always had but he'd always figured that when the time came to really go things would be different. Well they weren't. In fact they were worse. Now that he was gone for good and not just to Albuquerque his life ahead seemed suddenly as vast and empty as the desert and a little frightening. A person, he realized needs a person to talk to. Otherwise a person might just stop talking and one day wake up to find he'd upped and disappeared.

He started the engine and turned a U on the highway.

Marla was still sitting there drinking her Coke when he crossed the room again and sat down.

'Look,' he said, 'if I tell you will you promise not to laugh or nothing?'

She shrugged. She'd made a pyramid of the tapes, Alan Jackson on top.

'Promise?'

She shrugged again, but promised too.

'Well –' Jimmy paused. He'd never told a soul and his palms were sweating. He took a deep breath. 'I'm going to Tucson to join the Air Force.'

Marla looked up. 'Well I ain't going to Tucson,' she said. 'And I ain't joining no Air Force.'

'What?'

'I said I ain't joining no Air Force.'

Jimmy shook his head. He felt sick. Telling was a mistake. 'They ain't asking you,' he said.

'They asking you?'

He felt himself flushing. He thought of the letter he'd written and the letter he'd got in reply. It was a standard letter signed by the Chief Officer, Public Relations, thanking him for his interest in the United States Air Force.

'I got a letter,' he said limply.

Marla put down her Coke. 'Well, I got a letter from the President once but that don't make me no Kennedy.'

Jimmy stared at his hands. He was burning up, with rage, with embarrassment. He bit his lip, tasting blood. 'Well, I'm going,' he said. He didn't move.

'So go,' said Marla. 'I ain't stopping you.'

His hands found the sugar, turned it.

'Ain't you going?' she said.

'Sure I'm going.'

'Well?'

He pushed himself up. He looked over his shoulder at the parking lot, at the family's pick-up. He sat down again.

'You still here?' said Marla.

'Why're you going to Boulder?' he said.

'That's my business.'

'I told you mine.'

'So?'

'That was private too.'

'You told me. I didn't laugh. That was the deal. This is a different deal.'

'You going to see the dam?'

Marla shrugged. 'Maybe.'

'I ain't never seen the dam,' said Jimmy.

'Well, I ain't seen it neither.'

'They say it's big.'

'Big don't hardly cover it, I heard. I heard massive.'

'I seen the Empire State.'

'You ain't never.'

Jimmy flushed. It was a stupid lie. He never had been able to lie: his lies always got too big, out of hand. 'I seen pictures,' he said.

'Everybody's seen pictures.'

Across the room a man in a cowboy hat put a song on the jukebox: *Forever and Always Amen* by Randy Travis. Marla and Jimmy sat listening.

'You coming then?' said Jimmy when the record was through.

'Boulder?' said Marla.

Jimmy shrugged, looked down. 'Well, I ain't never seen the dam,' he said.

Marla sat a moment, then looked up at the boy. She felt a sudden sharp sadness at the giving up of dreams. 'Shoot, it's only a dam,' she said, pulling up a smile. 'You wanna go to Tucson? We'll go to Tucson.' She pushed herself out of the booth. 'I ain't never gave a damn about dams anyhow.'

52

THE WAY ETHAN remembered it, Vern had a way, when he was really angry (and Vern could get angry, make no mistake), of tapping his foot on the floor — just lightly — like he was keeping time with a song on the radio. He would stare at you, challenging, tapping away, until suddenly — seemingly for no reason at all — the moment passed and all was forgotten. There'd be games in the yard then and supper as usual and life would go on as before.

Or so he'd thought then.

Now he wasn't so sure.

All forgotten?

Maybe.

But maybe, he thought, as the miles rolled by beneath the Thunderbird's wheels, people never forget and never really forgive, and maybe a person's mistakes are always there to trip them and you're crazy if you think you can leave them behind. He looked at himself in the window's reflection. Crazy? Lately he'd got to thinking that maybe he was, or that maybe he was dreaming and was really sleeping and that any minute now he'd wake up in his bed and there at his side, lying in that way she had with her hands clasped together beside her head like an angel in prayer, would be his wife and all his hopes and he'd listen in the darkness to the sound of distant trains and not want to ride them and the sound through the wall of his deep-sleeping son. Sometimes it all seemed so close it was almost like being there again. Sometimes it was like everything in between — then to now — had never really existed, and that wisdom in those years — decades now — really had vanquished stupidity and selfishness and that running away with a hooker from Shreveport had been in itself just a dream or something he'd read in the

Bagdad Bugle and laughed at and not real life, at least not his life anyhow –

The Thunderbird ran wide on the highway, spitting stones. Jubal Early turned the wheel, correcting the swerve. He glanced over at the old man to see if the old man had noticed, but the old man was just looking out, a flat expression on his face like he'd lost ten dollars on a horse.

'You okay, sir?' he said.

Ethan said nothing. He felt suddenly tired. He closed his eyes. The car rumbled on.

When he woke it was evening. The car was off the highway, going slow. Up ahead were the lights of a motel.

'Where are we?' he said.

But Jubal Early was concentrating, pitched forward against the wheel, peering out at the gloom. 'Pardon me?' he said.

'I said where are we?'

He was frowning hard. 'Wikieup, I reckon. Leastways I ain't seen no other sign.' With a sly squeal of brakes the Thunderbird ground to a stop. Jubal Early pulled the shift to neutral and switched off the engine. He peered out at the motel's bank of neon. 'Pool,' he said, as if the word was new to him. He turned. 'That a game you like, sir – pool?'

'You don't play it,' said Ethan, 'you swim in it.'

Jubal Early frowned. You could almost see a thought cross his mind. 'Sir?' he said. 'Now I know we had a deal – don't think I don't – but may I ask you a question? It's just a tiny little question –'

Ethan sighed. 'What?'

'Well –' Jubal Early paused, looking suddenly nervous like a diver on the end of a board. 'Well, can you tell me is there darkness or light up there?'

'What?'

Jubal Early raised a finger towards the sky. 'In heaven,' he whispered.

Ethan Pierce shook his head.

'You mean there's neither?'

187

'You're mad – you know that?' he said.

Jubal Early nodded gravely. He'd heard this before. Madness, he'd heard, was a trait of the Earlys, from the earliest Early of all. 'Well,' he said sighing, 'I guess you'd be right not to say. We did have a deal and all.' With that he stepped out of the car and closed the door behind him. He walked slow through yellow neon to the motel's reception.

That evening they sat in the Santa Fe Suite watching TV and eating pizza. Neither man felt like talking. For Jubal Early talk of madness had drawn a melancholy over him and it was all he could do to eat. He watched the figures on the screen with a feeling of gloom, hardly stirring when the telephone rang. On the tenth ring he picked it up. 'Yes?' he said. It was the woman from reception: did Sir require an early call? 'No,' he said, then, too late, 'Thank you.' He replaced the receiver and looked over at the old man. The old man was lying on his bed snoozing, his mouth red with pizza. Jubal Early looked back at the TV. *Heavens,* said a man, as if reading his thoughts, *isn't madness passed down like the pigment of an eye?*

It was after ten when Ethan came to. The room was lit only by the light from the TV. He squinted in the gloom: the chair was empty – just a dip where a body had been. He pushed himself up and swung his legs round. His head was light; he sat still until it settled.

He tried the door but the door was locked. He waddled across the room and out onto the balcony thinking he might jump, but they were one storey up so that was out. He leaned against the railings and looked out at the lights. It was maybe Phoenix or Boulder far off, he couldn't say. He gazed up at the sky. The sky was full of stars. So much had happened – Perry Jemson's accident, the Pueblo, the flickering TV, being kidnapped by a loon – but none of it seemed real. He looked down at his bound hands as the echo of a thought came to him. Is there darkness or light? He frowned. For a second he remembered lying on a bed, feeling his life draining away, then everything fading, then everything gone. He rubbed his face, trying to drag out some sense, but sense wouldn't come. He peered again at his hands.

He was touching the TV, watching the channels flick around and around, when he heard the rattle of the bathroom door. He lifted his hands; the TV settled. He made his way back to the bed and lay down. He closed his eyes as a body passed by. The TV flicked off. There was darkness.

53

FROM THE MOMENT she stepped onto the floor of Vern's Bar and Grill, Tuesday Miller was a star and not only with the men but with the ladies too. She lit the place up like a dozen neon tubes, and even old Rod Mickelsson of Mickelsson's Mufflers had to agree she had something. Not one to praise easily, he said she had presence (he knew about these things, he said, owning as he did three muffler outlets in Las Vegas) and he stayed a time longer than he normally did. Normally on a Friday he was out of there by ten; by ten-thirty this Friday he was still drinking beer. By eleven he was standing swaying slightly by the jukebox. He punched in his coins and turned to the room. The room was full, the noise quite a level. He drew a deep breath and cradled his beer. There were tears in his eyes as he sang along:

> Oh I WANT you
> I NEED you
> I LUUURVE you

'Hey, Rod,' called a voice from the multitude, but Rod didn't hear, he just went on singing and was singing still when the record was through.

'Hey, Rod — that Tuesday you been singing to?'

Rod Mickelsson rubbed his eyes. He looked blearily about the room. A man not given to public performance, he was finding the experience a novel one. He grinned as the object of his passion passed by. He lunged amorously but tumbled, struck his head on a chair. Everything brightened then darkened to black. 'Kiss me,' were the last words he uttered that evening; in the morning he'd be sore as a bear.

*

'Well?' said Vern. 'How're y'all feeling?'

'Jesus, Vern,' said Marianne. She had her shoes off, was massaging her feet. It was two a.m. and the restaurant was closed. Tuesday and the other girls were sitting around, winding down, talking over the night. 'I sure hope you made enough to buy me them new shoes you been promising. I feel like I been walking to Texas and back. Say, you got that bottle?'

Vern paused in his counting and reached under the bar. It was a kind of tradition, drinking wine after a heavy night. 'White or red?'

'White,' said Laura. 'I hate red. You know I hate red, Vern.'

'Well I hate white,' said Alice. She looked down at her lap. 'White's like drinking, well, you-know-what.' She could feel herself blushing again. She always seemed to be blushing these days. She'd been to the doctor and the doctor had said it was hormones, which wasn't what she'd wanted to hear, and he'd given her pills, iron or something.

Vern placed two bottles, one red, one white, on the bar. 'Looks like it's your call, Tuesday,' he said. 'Tuesday?'

Tuesday was miles away. She looked up. 'What?'

'You okay, honey?' said Marianne. 'You wanna go home?'

'No, I'm fine.'

'You sure now?'

'Positive.' Tuesday smiled. She was clearly exhausted.

'Then you want a drink?' said Laura.

'I guess.'

'You want white wine?'

'I hate white wine,' said Alice, still looking down, still blushing. 'You know I hate white wine.' She was getting agitated and everyone knew when Alice got agitated things got broken. 'It tastes like –' She paused, teetering on the fine edge of rudeness.

Laura huffed. 'Like you-know-what?'

Then Alice looked up and somehow an ashtray lost its life, smashing into pieces at her feet.

'Jesus,' said Vern. 'Will you girls cut it out? What the hell will Tuesday be thinking of us now?'

'Well, *she* started it,' said Laura.

Vern raised a harsh brow. 'Enough, all right?' He could raise a harsh brow when required. 'Now,' he said, looking from one to the other, 'do you girls want to have a nice peaceful civilized drink or do you girls want to fight? Because if you want to fight then I suggest you go do your fighting some place else where they got a licence for fighting and on-hand medical attention, and that ain't here. Do I make myself clear?'

Laura shrugged. Alice looked down.

'Good,' said Vern. 'Now. Tuesday. Was it red or white?'

'Well —' said Tuesday. She glanced at Marianne who was smiling.

'You want pink?' said Marianne. Her smile made you want to smile back.

'I guess,' said Tuesday.

'I hate pink,' said Alice and Laura together and they stared at each other and then the moment slipped away and then everyone — them included — was laughing.

It was a little after three when Vern locked the door and switched off the lights. He made his way slow up the stairs.

The light was on in the bedroom but Clare was asleep. He switched off the light and took off his clothes, folding them neatly on a chair. He lay down in the moonlit room and closed his eyes. It had been a long night and he was ready for sleep.

But sleep wasn't ready for him. He punched his pillow and turned onto his side but it was no good. He lay awhile studying the shadows on the wall, his mind clicking round and round, first his father, then his girls, then Tuesday, then Clare. It was like he was standing in the middle of a fairground ride, watching them all riding by on gilt horses.

He eased himself up and stood at the window. When he couldn't sleep looking out at the lights of the town twinkling in the darkness usually fixed it. He'd think of all the people still up and working — the attendants at gas stations, the night staff at hotels — and more often than not thinking of their tiredness made him tired himself and ready again for sleep. But not tonight. Tonight the magic wouldn't work. Tonight all he could think of was his father in his grave and his children asleep in their beds. Tonight, more than ever before, he was aware of time passing: you could practically see it in the sky. He watched the clouds rolling slow across the moon, and the sky beyond the mountains already touched with pink. Soon it would be dawn. He turned away. In the street behind him a dog barked, and across town, at the dam, the vast weight of water sat still in the moonlight, poised behind its great wall of stone.

54

THE FIRST THEY saw of Tucson wasn't Tucson at all, it was just a band of purplish fog either side of the highway up ahead where the highway met the sky. To Marla it looked just like what you get when you get close to Vegas but she didn't say so as she knew how important Tucson being Tucson was to the boy, and besides she'd only ever seen Vegas in pictures so how could she really know? No, she just sat quiet and let the pick-up rumble on and went back to thinking how strange it was the way things change. Take her case, for instance. One minute she was stuck forever behind the counter at a truckstop Dairy Queen, then the next she was riding with Perry in his pick-up, not to mention an old man who was totally weird, and then –

She frowned.

'Hey, there it is,' said Jimmy. 'There's Tucson!'

She shrugged. She didn't like to think about *then*. *Then* was when things had started going wrong. *Then* was when she'd settled on jumping from the dam, which didn't explain what she was doing now riding shotgun with an Indian boy ten miles out of Tucson.

'Did you hear me?' said Jimmy.

'I heard you.'

'Well?'

'Well what?'

'Well, whaddaya think?'

She looked again at the purple haze. You could see the first signs of the city, buildings tall and glinting in the light. She thought about saying something sharp but then she said, 'Yeah, it's great, you must be real excited.'

The boy said nothing. Marla stole a glance. The boy was just staring ahead, sort of sullen. After what she'd said in the diner about not being a Kennedy just because she'd got a letter it was hardly surprising. She knew better than most how fragile dreams are. Though she didn't want to she thought again about Perry and wondered again where he was and she felt a sudden spurt of gloom. She looked out again at the scrub. The scrub was endless and depressed her. She'd always hated the desert (there'd been nothing to see from the Dairy Queen but endless miles of it) but now she hated it more. That was okay though – you don't *have* to like the desert – or would be if it weren't for the fact that she didn't really like cities much either (not that she had much experience of them, having only been to Flagstaff and Phoenix, but never properly, never to stay) and so sometimes it was hard to see herself happy and at home anyplace.

Maybe Tucson, she thought, as that city rose up, but even while she was thinking it and trying to get positive, even while she was smiling for the boy's sake at the city's towering buildings and streams of dusty cars, she couldn't help thinking that Tucson looked unlikely as a place to be happy, at least for her, and then maybe she didn't deserve to be happy anyhow, what with the way she'd conducted herself.

The boy slowed the pick-up into traffic.

'Well,' he said, 'I guess this is it.' He sounded nervous. He was looking straight ahead. 'You reckon there'll be a sign?'

Marla shrugged.

The car in front moved; before Jimmy could find a gear the car behind honked. 'Jesus,' he said. He ground the shift. The pick-up objected, rolled on.

55

CLARE PIERCE WAS in the office working on the monthly account-
ing when the telephone rang. She paused, holding her pen
halfway down a column of figures, and picked up the phone.
'Yes?'

'Is that Vern's Bar and Grill?'

'It is.' She was frowning at the figures, as usual they weren't
adding. 'May I help you?'

'Well –'

Two and twelve and twenty and thirteen: how on earth did
Vern get to sixty-one? 'Was it about the ad?' she said. Three calls
so far had been about the ad, it seemed the town right now was
full of out-of-work waitresses.

'The ad?'

She drew a line through the total at the foot of the column.
'It's gone,' she said.

'What?'

'The position. Waitress. You *were* calling about the ad?'

There was silence down the line.

'Hello?'

'I don't know nothing about no ad. I'm calling about Vern.'

She set down her pen.

'Well, about Ethan actually.'

'Ethan? What about him?'

More silence, the faint chatter of a TV.

Clare sighed. 'Look, who is this? Is this some kind of joke?'

'He's not dead.'

'I beg your pardon?'

'Ethan. He's alive. He got struck by lightning, see –'

Clare felt her spirits dip. 'Look,' she said, 'I don't know who you are but whoever you are I suggest you seek some kind of medical assistance —'

'What?'

'You heard me.'

'But it's true!'

'A psychiatrist, for example, preferably one in another state, okay?'

'But —'

Clare set down the phone, as, nearly two hundred miles away, did Virginia Brinkman. She was sitting with her sister in the parlour of their late daddy's home.

'Well?' said Dorothy. The idea to ring up hadn't been hers: just to let things lie, in time to be forgotten, had been her wishes on the matter. Let the stupid old fool run off if he wanted to, and good riddance to him.

Virginia shrugged.

'Told you,' said Dorothy. There was no way she was running after him — and no way she'd have her sister running either. She pushed herself up. 'That's an end of it,' she said solemnly, gripping the mantelpiece in the manner of their father. She looked hard at Virginia. 'Well?'

Virginia said nothing.

'Ginny — did you hear me?'

'I heard you,' she said. She pushed out her lips. Long ago she'd decided that life wasn't fair, specially when there's sisters involved. In an act of defiance unheard by her sister, she raised herself slightly and broke silent wind.

56

THE TRUTH WAS Marla couldn't get out of her head the fact that she had to have done something wrong to have made Perry take off like he did. But she couldn't think what: had she come on too strong or not strong enough? Should she have done something different and if so — what? It's hard to know you've done something wrong but not to know what it is, because if you don't know what it is, what's to say you won't go and do it again next time? Not that Marla was expecting a next time, no sir. She'd had her time and she'd wasted it. You don't get two times with a person like Perry, that was for sure, certain like a rule of life.

'You see anything yet?' said Jimmy.

They were deep in the city now, emerging into sun from the darkness of an underpass. Marla looked around. It looked like downtown — office blocks, commuters, Tucson Savings and Loan. 'Ain't you got that letter?' she said. 'Some address? I mean we ain't gonna find no airport round here.'

'Field,' said Jimmy.

'What?'

'Air*field*, not air*port* —'

'Well, whatever.' Marla squinted out at the buildings. Thinking about Perry had got her depressed and being depressed had got her spiky: she hated that she'd messed up her one chance with Perry and thinking about it made her feel kind of sick. 'So you got that letter or not?' she said, real spiky.

Jimmy shrugged. They were running out of downtown now and into suburban, wide streets, residential. A sign overhead read Malls Next Exit.

'Please yourself,' said Marla. 'I just thought you wanted to find the place is all.'

'Well, I do,' said Jimmy, he was still staring straight ahead.

'Sure you do.'

He turned. 'What's that supposed to mean?'

'Nothing,' said Marla, though nothing wasn't it and Jimmy knew it, he knew he was flushing and not just from the heat.

'You think I don't wanna find it?' he said. 'You think I'm scared?'

Marla shrugged.

''Cause I ain't. I ain't. You know that?'

'I know that,' said Marla, though what she really knew was how scary it is getting close to your dreams, in case those dreams turn out bad or blow up in your face like the Perry thing had blown up in hers. 'It's okay,' she said.

Jimmy said nothing. He gripped the wheel. 'I ain't scared,' he said at last. They drove on.

57

OF THE TWO things Ethan Pierce knew he had to get thought
about that morning and fast – Boulder City being less than a
hundred miles off – the first was too big and the second too
weird to make thinking about them easy; in fact, ever since
they'd rumbled out of Phoenix heading for Flag, what with the
bigness of one thing and the weirdness of the other and the
driver's driving, which was either way too fast or way too slow
but either way scarifying, he'd managed to get just about no
thinking done. He'd spent his time gripping his seat with his
bound hands and turning into bends as if arching his back might
help and listening to the driver's strange humming. It was a
nervous kind of humming and made him nervous too, which was
just exactly what he didn't need. What a man needs who's not
seen his family for the best part of twenty years and is just about
to, not to mention a man who, weird as it might seem, might just
have come back from the dead or be senile enough to even think
that he had, is calmness, a silence conducive to thinking, which
was not what he was getting, which was humming, endless,
tuneless humming, the sort of humming a person would go live
in Baltimore to avoid, which of course he couldn't. In fact he
could hardly move at all, what with the gathering stiffness in his
limbs and the string around his wrists and ankles. All he could do
was watch the road ahead and listen, watch the signs as they
flicked or dragged by.

'You alright?' said Jubal Early, quitting humming long enough
to ask the question. They were crawling in the outside lane
behind a horse-box and trailer. He was fishing about in the box
for a gear. 'You know we can talk if you want to. I like to talk.
You want to talk?'

'I want to think,' said Ethan.

'Alright,' said Jubal Early, grinding a gear, pulling out, the engine raving, 'I like to think too!' In a moment they were rattling and banging past the horse-box. 'You know what I was thinking?' He had to shout above the noise.

Ethan looked out, straight into the eyes of the driver of the car that was pulling the trailer. The driver was smiling, raising a hand, one finger extended. Ethan looked away. The world sometimes was a depressing place. 'What?' he said, heaven knows why.

'I was thinking about you and me.'

'What?'

Jubal Early shrugged. He seemed to be driving with greater confidence now, though he was no better at it. 'Well, I was thinking about how we're kind of getting along now —'

Jesus, thought Ethan.

'And I was thinking about how maybe we should start talking about stuff — like colors maybe. You like colors? I mean do you like any one color more than the rest?' He glanced over at Ethan and the Thunderbird swerved. 'I like blue best. You have one favorite color?'

It was then, when his captor began revealing the details of his life — his favorite foods, the way as a boy he'd never liked bubble gum, especially the way it got stuck in your braces — that Ethan Pierce knew that time was running out. He had to get thinking, had to figure out not only what was happening but also what it was he was planning to say. He closed his eyes, feigning sleep. He wrenched his mind round to Vern. In his mind Vern was smiling as he had as a boy. He'd not be smiling soon.

'How about oatcakes?' said Jubal Early, but Ethan settled back, made a play of snoozing sleep. In his mind he was standing at a window in Shreveport, his shirt hanging loose and no pants; below in the street was Vern looking up, come his one and only time to patch things up, but to no avail, to just shouting in the street, to stabbing fingers, hurtful words. Ethan squirmed at the memory. What could he say that would make up the time? He opened his eyes and Shreveport faded. There was nothing left, the time was gone.

'Stop the car,' he said.

Jubal Early looked over. He'd been cranking up the speed, getting ready to heave past a U-Haul box trailer. 'Stop?' he shouted, hard above the noise. 'Did you say stop?'

Ethan Pierce nodded, looked away. He studied the scrub in the fields below the highway, and it came to him now without any alarm that it was here in the bleakness of the Arizona desert that he'd probably be meeting his end. He felt the car weave, spitting stones on the shoulder. It ground to a stop, was still.

'What is it?' said Jubal Early. 'Ain't you feeling too good? I know when I'm driving I sometimes get to feeling real kind of unsettled, it's the movement –'

Ethan shook his head. 'I ain't sick,' he said. 'And I ain't going on. So you can do what you like.'

For a moment Jubal Early was silent, thinking, then he said, 'You mean you don't wanna go to Boulder City?'

'That's what I said.'

He looked suddenly grave. 'But we had a deal.'

'So shoot me. I know you're gonna anyhow.'

'I ain't gonna shoot you.'

'So what you gonna do?'

Well this really stumped Jubal Early. In his mind he'd had them coming to a stop in Boulder City, then doing the deal and parting like friends. But now this.

'I know you're *mean*,' said Ethan, hardly caring what he said now. 'I know you're gonna do *something*, *mean* man like you. Well ain't you?' He studied Jubal Early's pale face and the youth and indecision within it and it occurred to him that he was really only a boy, maybe twenty, twenty-two. 'Who *are* you?' he said. 'What are you doing?'

Jubal Early looked up. 'Driving you to Boulder. Leastways I was –'

'Why?'

'Well I don't know, it's you as said Boulder –'

Ethan Pierce shook his head. 'No, I mean why all this –' He raised his bound hands. 'What is it you want?'

'I want your story,' said Jubal Early.

'My story? What story?'

He shrugged. 'Well, what it was like to die and come back, of course, what it was like in heaven. The public likes to learn these things, so as they can prepare –'

Ethan Pierce felt suddenly light-headed. He thought about lying in the darkness of his room and fading, he thought about the flickering TVs. He looked down at his hands, heard himself saying, 'You mean I really was dead?'

'I guess,' said Jubal Early.

'You guess?'

He shrugged. 'Well, your heart sure had stopped. I heard people fixing to bury you alright –' Jubal Early stopped himself as an unpleasant thought crossed his mind. He narrowed his eyes. 'You mean you don't remember nothing?'

Ethan Pierce shook his head.

'Not even getting struck by lightning?'

He shook his head again.

'Nothing at all?'

People fixing to bury you. Ethan rubbed his face, trying to squeeze out a memory, but none came. There was nothing, a blank.

'Not even the tiniest thing?'

'Look,' said Ethan, 'I told you. Nothing.' He looked at Jubal Early.

Jubal Early was squinting, biting his lip, thinking. He thought about the chisel but at once dismissed it: what a man doesn't know a man can't reveal.

'Well? What you gonna do?'

'Well,' he said, stalling. Then playing for time he said, 'Why Boulder?'

'What?'

'Why'd you wanna go there?'

'I told you, I don't.'

'But you did.'

203

Ethan Pierce turned away and in the moment of his turning Jubal Early saw that all was not lost: there are stories in secrets and this man, it was clear, had a secret. He fed his hand beneath the wheel and twisted the Thunderbird's key.

Ethan looked back, his face was pale. 'What are you doing?' he said. 'Where're we going?'

Jubal Early gripped the wheel. He smiled. 'Boulder,' he said, then, liking its sound, he said it again and again.

58

THE 57TH TACTICAL AIR WING, Tucson, Arizona, lay some ways off the highway when they first caught sight of it, its long low sand-colored buildings and lines of neatly-parked planes shimmering in the heat off the desert like some military mirage. There was a single taller building and here and there a patch of grass, the tiny finger of a flagpole, a slow-moving truck, a stationary car.

The pick-up slowed and stopped on the dirt.

'Well,' said Marla and she was going to say more like how big it was and other stuff but something made her stop, a sense of the solemness of the moment or something. She glanced at the boy. 'You okay?'

But Jimmy Chai was just staring, his chin on his arms and his arms folded over the wheel. He had a look in his eye that made Marla think of folks in a church, weddings or funerals, and she just turned away and sat looking too, and they sat that way for maybe an hour while the sun overhead arched its tangent in the sky.

It was two o'clock nearly when Jimmy stirred. His arms were stiff, he rubbed his eyes with the tips of his fingers. Marla sat up too and Jimmy said, 'You wanna go now?' as if all the time he'd been waiting for her.

She shrugged. 'I guess,' she said, and then she said, 'Jimmy?' It was the first time she'd said his name.

'What?'

'What were you thinking about?'

'When?'

'Just now.'

'I don't know.'

'You must know.'

'Well I don't.'

She shrugged again, looked out. 'You know what I was thinking? I was thinking about flying, being up there flying around, looking down on you and me sitting in this pick-up like we was waiting for the lights or something – were you thinking that?' She turned to see Jimmy shaking his head but not in a bad way like he was mocking her but in a nice way like they were just two friends talking. 'You weren't thinking that?' she said.

'Nope,' said Jimmy.

'So what *were* you thinking?'

'I told you, I don't know.'

'Sure you do. Everybody knows what they're thinking.'

'Well I don't.'

'I mean I *know* what I'm thinking right now – don't you?'

'What?'

'I'm thinking that maybe if you join the Air Force I might join the Air Force too.'

'You?'

'Why not? Don't they have lady pilots?'

'No,' said Jimmy. 'They don't.'

'You're lying,' said Marla.

'I'm not!'

'You *are*, you're blushing –'

Jimmy turned away.

'And besides, *you* may not know what you're thinking, but *I* know what you're thinking –'

He turned back. 'Oh? And what's that?'

Well here goes, thought Marla. 'You're thinking no way am I ever gonna let a lady who's gonna be a pilot give *me* a kiss –'

'What?'

And then she did it, she leaned right over and planted a kiss as big as Texas on his cheek. 'There!' she said proudly.

'What was that for?' Jimmy Chai was rubbing his cheek as if she'd slapped him not kissed him.

'For luck.'

'What for?'

'For flying, of course. Ain't you gonna say thank you?'

'I don't need luck,' said Jimmy.

'Oh, everybody needs luck. Just as everybody gets scared.'

He looked up. 'I said I ain't scared and I ain't.'

'I get scared all the time,' said Marla.

'Well, I don't.'

'Never? Ain't you never got scared?'

Jimmy shrugged.

Marla spread her hands out on the dash and studied them. 'You know what scares me?' she said.

'What?'

She curled her fingers and straightened them.

'What?' said Jimmy.

'You promise you won't laugh?'

Jimmy shrugged, promised.

'What scares me is I'm forty-nine years old this January and I'm maybe never gonna get married –'

'I ain't getting married,' said Jimmy.

'And I ain't never gonna be a wife and have some nice place instead of some lousy place and I ain't never gonna have three kids and have one of them break his finger like I broke my finger and come to me so as I can make it better and have a husband who loves me and brings me things instead of them creeps that just whistle and whine –'

'Hey, Marla,' said Jimmy.

'What?' She was wiping her eyes.

'You really gonna be a pilot?'

'Why – don't you think I should?'

'I don't know.'

'I guess they won't take kindly to crying pilots.'

'I guess not.'

'I guess I better straighten myself up, huh?'

Jimmy shrugged. He was running his finger real slow round the wheel. He stopped. 'Can I ask you something?'

'What?'

'Well, do you think its weird if a person gets scared of what they want? Like you get scared that if you actually get something then you ain't gonna want it and that maybe you been thinking you want something you don't really want and you just like thinking about it?'

'Nah, that ain't weird,' said Marla.

'You don't reckon?'

'I don't reckon. You know what?'

'What?'

'I reckon it don't mean a person don't really want it neither, but maybe they just don't want it now, maybe it just ain't right now, that maybe a person's got to put in the training first before they start flying –'

'You mean like school?' said Jimmy.

'Yeah, like school, and other stuff like families. You got a family?'

'I got two brothers.'

'You got a mother?'

Jimmy nodded.

'I guess she'll be real worried by now.'

He shrugged. 'I guess. You think I should call her?'

'Well, that's up to you, but if I was your mother I'd sure be glad if you called me –'

'Well, maybe I should,' said Jimmy. He was gripping the wheel. 'I ain't quitting, though. I'm still gonna fly, okay?'

'Okay,' said Marla, 'I'll make you a deal. You don't quit getting ready to fly and I won't quit getting ready to find me a husband. That a deal?' She held out her hand.

'Deal,' said Jimmy, and for the first time Marla Thomson saw him smile and it was a wonderful smile, a smile as broad as the broad Colorado and as warm as the warm desert winds.

He dropped her at the Greyhound in downtown Phoenix and she waved as he drove off into traffic. She watched him until he was gone.

Despite the heat of the day it was cool on the concourse and she pulled her jacket tight around her. The place was busy, people bustling to and fro, arriving, departing, and though they jostled her as they passed she didn't mind, it was good to be where things were happening. She watched a man loaded down with bags light a cigarette then pass it to a woman in a hat and she smiled at a child who just stared at her and didn't smile back, but she didn't take offence. She listened to a voice overhead announcing times and destinations and she thought, *I could go anywhere.*

She heard the concourse clock strike four as she stood in a queue at a ticket window. She listened to the talk around her. *Cleveland*, people said, and *Kansas* and *New York City* and *Baton Rouge* and *Salt Lake City*. She gazed up at a poster of the Golden Gate Bridge. *I could go anywhere*, she thought.

'Yes, ma'am?'

She looked down at the nudge of an arm. The man behind the counter was smiling and for a moment Marla thought it was Perry.

'Ma'am?'

But then she saw the man's moustache and the darkness of his eyes and it came to her only then as she watched his lips moving that she really had nowhere to go.

The ticket-man leaned forward. 'Ma'am? Can I help you, ma'am?'

She looked down at her hands, at the ringless third finger, and she thought about the boy, about the Dairy Queen, about Perry, and a weariness with living crept around her like a mist. Then, her voice like a voice in a dream, she whispered the name of a city in the west and listened while the ticket-man said it back. She nodded. She watched her hands opening her purse, passing money through the window.

The man stamped a ticket, passed it through. 'Gate six,' he said. 'Leaves in an hour. You have a nice day now, y'hear?'

59

IT WAS WEIRD but from the moment they passed over the line
and into the outskirts of Boulder Ethan Pierce felt like he'd been
there before, which he hadn't. He hadn't even seen pictures, at
least none he could remember, except for the pictures he'd
started seeing in his mind (which were really just imaginings)
when Shreveport and Audacity had started losing their gloss and
he'd taken to spending more nights than he had to on the road in
the kind of motels where the TVs never work and the beds are
so dippy it's real hard to sleep. He'd lie awake nights just
imagining Boulder City, its neat little streets and lines of clean
cars and cut lawns and fences and he'd feel an ache in his heart
and so lonesome that he'd have to start drinking to stand any
chance of sleeping, which was part of the problem in the first
place, the drinking that is. It was drinking (directly or indirectly,
he couldn't remember now) that had led him from home and into
the arms of Audacity, and drinking and foolishness that had led
him to here, to a seat in a beat-up Thunderbird, to his arms and
legs tied, to the company of a man who was perfectly mad, to
the streets of a city he'd dreamed of and dreaded.

'You see that?' said Jubal Early. They were cruising down a
wide street between lines of parked cars. 'You reckon there's
some kind of party going on?' The street-lights were coming on,
people moving to and fro. There were bows on the trees and
bunting overhead.

Ethan Pierce said nothing. He'd been saying nothing for three
hours and he didn't feel like starting now. What he felt like doing
was getting out and running but that wasn't an option, so he just
settled on silence and staring out and wondering what on earth
was going to happen. Sooner or later he'd have to say something,

have to make something up about why he'd chosen Boulder of all places, but right now he couldn't figure anything – right now he couldn't even figure the truth. Okay, so he'd figured maybe getting to the city and getting to his son had meant some kind of protection, but was that sensible? Was it hell! Wouldn't Vern just say Go Ahead Shoot Him, not to mention that wife of his who'd always considered her father-in-law only second to Richard Nixon in the man-you-wouldn't-trust-with-a-bagful-of-dimes stakes? Sure they would, and in his heart he couldn't blame them. And then there was the little matter of his (maybe) having been dead and (maybe) getting struck by lightning and (maybe) being alive again, and even if that wasn't true (it *was* ludicrous alright), his even considering it meant at the very least he was half senile which they'd see and which would give them the water-tight reason they'd been looking for for sending him off into the care of the state where he'd soon be dribbling and soon have lost those of his marbles that still remained. No, either way you looked at it, he had to think of something and fast – but what?

The car slowed at lights. Ethan watched gloomily as a middle-aged couple crossed the street hand in hand. Maybe he could say that it was fear that had made him pick Boulder City at random or that maybe he'd always had a thing about dams? He glanced at Jubal Early, weighing these explanations, but Jubal Early was just staring straight, his features still, inscrutable. Ethan looked away, back out at the street. Any moment, he thought, there it'll be – Vern's Bar and Grill. He eased himself down in the seat. Time was running out. He had to think fast.

Sandwiched between Luigi Luigi's Italian Restaurant and the Day-2-Day Cleaners, the Hoover Motel on Arizona Street you reached by steering through an archway and into a courtyard in the center of which raised up was the motel's famous swimming-pool. The swimming-pool was famous as being the body of water in which on the day of the dam's inauguration fifty years ago a child and its mother had drowned. Following the tragedy (the result, all agreed, of a mother's inattention) the pool was emptied and never refilled; it was empty still that fine summer's evening as Jubal Early drew Horace Pico's old Thunderbird to a stop.

'There we are, sir,' he said, twisting the key. The car grumbled and died. He looked over. 'You okay, sir?' For three hours he'd been trying to figure out how best to proceed, and seeing as how he'd tried threatening and threatening hadn't worked, he figured it was down to cajoling which, having the nature he had, didn't exactly come natural, but then he didn't exactly have a choice did he? So cajoling it was. 'I was thinking,' he said, injecting as best he could a note of lightness in his voice. He paused, glanced over. 'Can you guess what I was thinking, sir?' he said.

Ethan Pierce said nothing.

'Well,' said Jubal Early, pressing on, 'I was thinking perhaps we could have ourselves a swim. Perhaps a lesson? Would you teach me to dive, sir?'

'It's empty,' said Ethan. He thought about explaining about Marjorie Loopswill and little Annabelle but then he thought, *Why should I?* Instead he just held up his bound hands and said, 'What about these?'

Jubal Early considered the hands, the wrists, the bindings. He'd feared all along that cajoling alone might not be enough and that the old man would demand complete liberation as the price for revealing what he had to reveal. 'You ain't gonna run away?' he said.

'What if I do?' said Ethan. 'You gonna hit me with your chisel?' He stared at Jubal Early whose color for the first time was rising. 'Well?'

'I ain't gonna hit you,' said Jubal Early. 'I ain't the hitting type. Don't you know that by now?'

Ethan Pierce shrugged, looked out to the courtyard. He felt suddenly so weary with thinking, with everything, so burdened with Shreveport and Audacity and with the whole solid weight of the past, that all he wanted to do now was to let it all go, get it all out of him and then maybe sleep for a week or a month, that he scarcely heard the rustling of the figure beside him, or the clipping of scissors in the gathering dusk.

60

FIRST A TRICKLE, then a flood, and soon he couldn't talk fast enough as all the pressure to tell that had built up over years was released and all the voices and faces kept for so long in darkness stepped into the light. There was Vern and Audacity and Shreveport and Clare and a family and a wife abandoned – so much to atone for, so much guilt, so much regret that there were times in the darkness when he could feel it all rising up nearly ready to swamp him, but still he kept on, articulating everything, leaving nothing unsaid, until hours had passed and there was no more to say and the room and Ethan fell into grateful silence.

In a while Jubal Early said, 'Are you okay, sir?' and Ethan turned his head. Jubal Early was sitting in the window with his notebook, as dark in the darkness as a priest. Ethan squinted, trying to make the figure out, but soon he was drifting, his limbs as light as air, his eyes heavy and falling.

When he woke the room was black, there was no moon now. He pushed himself up. 'Hello?' he said. The chair was empty. He lay back down, closed his eyes, listened to the nightsounds, to the chatter of voices and the hissing of cars in the street, and he was struck then in the darkness by the distance he'd traveled, Wilcox to Shreveport to Bagdad to here, and how he'd come so far just to wind up alone. He turned in the gloom to the window. His heart was racing, it was unstable now like maybe soon it would stop altogether, and he felt the time to make amends fast running out. He stared at the curtains: there were hours still before dawn. He listened to the barking of a faraway dog and prayed with all his might for the daylight's advance.

At first Tuesday Miller thought the man with the pale face and

213

214

pale blue eyes was some kind of preacher, maybe from one of them real weird sects, she reckoned, but then when she took his order and his order was the steak dinner and a bottle of Bud she knew he was just weird and not part of a sect necessarily, except maybe a sect of one, that is.

'He sure is a spook all right,' said Marianne, peering through the kitchen door. Marianne knew about spooks on account of her having married one and having had one for a daddy. 'What's he ordering?'

'Steak and Bud,' said Tuesday.

'And he ain't said nothing? You ain't felt a hand? Guys like him got more hands than a battleship, you better know that –'

'He just said he's obliged.'

'Obliged? What for is he obliged?'

Tuesday shrugged, she glanced at her watch.

'You okay, honey?'

'I'm fine,' she said, though what with the anniversary tomorrow and all the extra business and Alice being off with a broken finger and all, not to mention the fact that all this walking and standing wasn't a bit like working for Elvis and was giving her blisters, she felt like maybe she should go sit down for a bit and maybe get her breath back but she didn't dare to there being all these people and besides if she did she'd probably never get up again.

'You sure now?' said Marianne.

'Positive,' said Tuesday, and together the two girls pushed through the doors and onto the floor of the restaurant.

'Where you been?'

'Dancing,' said Jubal Early.

'Dancing?'

He flicked on a lamp. The old man flinched as if the sudden light were painful. The old man looked suddenly older now, ancient, fragile. 'You hungry?'

Ethan Pierce shook his head. His eyes were squinty, his face dead pale. 'You see him?' he said.

'Who?'

214

'You know.'

Jubal Early drew a large piece of steak from his pocket; from the other he pulled out a bottle of beer. These he placed on the table. 'You know what I reckon?' he said.

'What?'

'I reckon you don't eat you ain't gonna live. Ain't nobody gonna live if they don't eat.'

'I ain't hungry,' said Ethan. 'Just awful tired.' He lay back. He was quiet then for so long Jubal Early thought he was asleep, but then he said, '*Did* you see him?'

'You mean Vern?'

'Well, did you?'

'I saw him.'

'And?'

'Well,' said Jubal Early. 'Seems to me like the man's been waiting. Seems to me like he's ready for his daddy.' He glanced over at the old man to see if he'd picked out the lie, but the old man was out now, hands parked across his chest, looking there for all the world like a body lying still on a tomb.

61

IT WAS DAYLIGHT when the bus pulled up. The doors hissed and some people got out. Those with bags to collect hung about by the bus waiting for the driver. Marla just walked away.

'You know where you're going, honey?'

She didn't slow down, didn't turn around.

'I mean you look kinda lost –'

'I ain't lost,' she said. A hand touched her elbow; she pulled away. All night since Montesuma, Mr Bell ('Call me Bob') had been rattling out the whole story of his life, his job selling auto parts, his kids, his wife, and even when he'd slept for an hour out of Phoenix he'd snored so bad she'd half wished he was talking instead.

She turned a corner; he turned it too. She quickened her pace and in a while he fell back. She slowed, walked on, looked back. He was standing on the corner, a tiny figure now, rippling like some kind of alien in the heat off the road.

She didn't know where she was going but she kept walking anyhow, she reckoned you can't miss a dam. Every corner she turned she figured she'd see it but she didn't. She paused now and then, listening for water.

By seven she was tired and thirsty. She crossed the street to a burger stand and bought a can of soda which she drank in one. 'Man,' said the vendor, watching her go. She didn't respond, didn't even hear him.

The closer she got to the center of town the more she noticed the decorations. It was like the place was gearing up for a party: there were bows on the trees and banners overhead that said HAPPY BIRTHDAY TO THE DAM and streamers hanging down in the morning heat.

All night on the bus she'd tried to but she couldn't stop thinking – about Perry, about the boy, about Duane and his ring and the Dairy Queen. It was like they were traveling with her wherever she went, no matter how many miles she covered or how many times she told herself they were gone and she'd never see any of them again. It was like there was this little piece of hope left inside her which plain refused to get dead and though she'd tried to ignore it it wouldn't be ignored. It kept chattering away like some tiny little person of its own, except that you couldn't walk away from it like you could a real person, a person on a bus for instance.

'The dam?'

She was standing on the sidewalk peering into the darkness of a police car. The man at the wheel was smiling, eyes creasing up behind his shades. 'Which dam would that be, ma'am?'

'Boulder Dam,' said Marla.

'Uh-huh. You got business there, ma'am?'

Marla Thomson looked hard into the center of the man's glasses. His smile took a dip. 'I'm planning to jump,' she said calmly.

The policeman looked across at his partner then back.

'Did you say jump?'

'I did.'

'You feeling okay, ma'am?'

Marla Thomson shrugged. She felt okay, a little light-headed maybe. Nothing seemed real.

Except the back of the police car was real and the way they drove slow through the streets. She gazed through the mesh at the back of their heads and thought about maybe what she'd do if she was a hairdresser, which of course she wasn't.

She could tell the car was slowing by a shift in her stomach, and then she was walking down a brightly-lit corridor, then smiling at a man who was smiling at her. He asked her her name and she told him, and her date of birth and other things, and then he asked her if she was feeling okay and she said okay but a little light-headed. Then she was lying down in a cool room, looking up at the cracks in the plaster.

Then just as fast she was out on the street, the sun was high now, blazing. She moved across the street and in through a door. It was a bank. She watched her feet stepping up to a counter. 'Excuse me,' she heard herself saying. 'Has anybody seen the dam?'

62

ETHAN DRESSED IN SILENCE and when he was done he took some
paper from the bathroom and did the best he could to polish up
Judge Brinkman's old sentencing shoes which, though they were
older even than the dam, were still in pretty good shape. And
when this was done and he'd tied the laces and pulled up his
socks so they didn't ride down, he took a minute with himself in
the mirror, just hoping to find he didn't look quite as old as he
felt, which he did, in fact he looked older. He felt about a
hundred but he looked about a hundred and fifty, and tired also.
He felt so awful weary that he had to sit down on the tub before
his legs gave from under him, and he was still sitting there when
there came a tapping on the door.

'You okay in there, sir?'

'I'm feeling my age and it don't feel good,' he said, and he felt as
he said it like he might never get up and the janitor or somebody
was gonna have to break in the door and be faced with the nightmare of a seven-stone man who seemed to like dying so much
he'd gone and done it twice. 'Besides,' he said, he was gripping
the tub trying to work up some strength, 'I ain't in no hellfire
hurry. I ain't seen none of them in the best part of twenty years
so I reckon a few damn seconds ain't gonna make no difference.'

'Okay,' said Jubal Early. He paused, listening at the door, and
Ethan could tell he was listening.

'What the hell're you doing?' he said.

'Doing? I ain't doing nothing.'

At last he pushed himself up. He was still swaying some, but a
little steadier. 'Can't a man even take a piss around here without
an audience? I said I ain't hurrying and I ain't, so leave me be,
alright?'

'Alright,' said Jubal Early. 'But you are coming out, ain't you?'

'Of course I'm coming out!'

'All right then.' Jubal Early moved away, paused. 'It's ten forty-one mind. Will you mind that fact?'

Ethan Pierce said nothing. He slumped back down on the tub. The truth was right now he didn't know if he *could* leave the room and not just because he felt so damn old and like he was about to collapse or something but because of Vern and Clare and how they'd hate him now if they ever thought of him at all, which they probably wouldn't, seeing as how they thought he was dead. Which was another thing: what the hell was gonna happen when he pushed on that door and there he was standing being looked at by people who'd last seen him dead as Elvis in a box? He just couldn't imagine and that was the truth, it was just a blank, a hole in his mind which if he tried to fill just got him scared and shaking like he was shaking now. He closed his eyes and tried to breathe himself calm, but that was like asking a man to be calm that's standing on a ledge on the Empire State Building, which given the way he was feeling he might just as well have been.

There came another tap.

'What now?' he said.

'Ain't you coming?'

'I said I'm coming, didn't I?'

'Well, are you coming today or in time for Thanksgiving?'

Jesus Christ. He pushed himself up again and this time made it over to the door, which he opened and stuck his head out of. 'Who the hell are you anyway?' he said, but to an empty room. The room door was open, outside in the courtyard was the sound of a car starting up. 'What the hell're you doing?' he called but it was no good, there was nothing to do now but what had to be done. He picked up his cap and made his way through the door.

Outside the sun was blazing and for a moment Ethan was blind, and in that moment of blindness he thought he saw God and God in His heaven was considering His watch, tapping its face and frowning at the time.

63

IT WAS JUST MARLA'S LUCK that the bank she walked into, the First National Bank of Nevada on Main Street, had as its manager a man named Bob who that morning had just bussed in from Phoenix and to whom the cutting edge of humor was a man in his position pretending to be an out-of-state trader in auto parts.

'Well,' he said, heels clipping the bright floor, advancing towards her. 'If it ain't my companion Miss Silent —'

'What?' said Marla. The bright floor was dazzling.

Bob Bell mock-frowned. 'Ah, now surely you ain't saying you forgot?'

Marla stared hard at the man's florid face. It meant nothing to her. 'I'm sorry,' she said. 'I'm looking for the dam. Do you know where that is?'

'Well I surely do,' said Bob Bell. 'Are you looking to celebrate?'

'I'm looking to jump,' said Marla, aware of her own voice echoing.

For a moment Bob Bell, Ace King of Humor, wasn't sure she was joking and then he was sure and he laughed from his gut like he'd laughed at Jerry Lewis as a boy. 'Jump off?' he managed when the first tide had passed and his eyes were full of water and his cheeks were redder still. He shook his head, he was dabbing his head with a handkerchief. 'You got one of them bungee things?' he said.

'What?' said Marla. She was thinking the man might just burst if he got any redder.

'You gonna do one of them bungee jumps like they do in Australia?'

Marla Thomson shook her head. 'I don't know nothing about that,' she said. 'I'm just looking for the dam.'

'Right,' said Bob Bell, and suddenly the Ace King of Humor was no longer laughing, in fact he was thinking about calling security as the woman before him was quite clearly mad.

'Well, do you?' she said. 'Know where it is, I mean?'

He glanced over her shoulder and with the wink of an eye had a man in a uniform and peaked cap stepping over. 'Yes, sir?' said the guard, not looking at Marla. 'Is there trouble, sir?'

'This lady,' said Bob Bell, 'was just on her way. Would you render her some assistance?'

The man in the uniform gripped Marla by the arm and soon she was out on the street. She turned, bemused, to look back at the bank, but all she could see was the sunlight on the glass, so harsh it burned her eyes and turned her away, and soon she was drifting in and out of the crowds, her hand shielding her eyes and her ears once again tuned to water.

64

IT WAS ONLY A BLOCK, but to Ethan it seemed more like ten and not just because of Jubal Early's woeful driving, which seemed if anything worse than ever now, particularly in the steering and braking and accelerating departments, which was pretty much all the departments that mattered, but also because – perhaps more because – he had this real strong feeling that Vern was gonna go tell him jump, after he'd picked himself up from fainting, that is, and after Clare had kicked his ass (she was a tough woman, Clare, at least in his memory) about as far as a woman can kick an old man, which is one hell of a long way. So to say he was nervous would be accurate but not as accurate as to say he was scared to the point of being somewhat light-headed which, allied to his age which was high and his strength which was low, all made up a package of one squitty old man. And then as if all that weren't enough there were all these people just milling about, more than enough to make a squitty old man who was already nervous get real nervous.

'What the hell's going on?' he said. 'Who *are* all these people?'

Jubal Early shrugged. He'd been trying to find second gear but instead he'd found fourth and the Thunderbird was labouring like a turtle up a beach. He applied the brakes abruptly at a stop-light and sat back, grateful for a moment's intermission. Not turning his head (stop-lights in his experience were quixotic things and demanded much attention) he said, 'Pardon me, sir?' but Ethan Pierce wasn't listening, being more concerned now looking out for a certain Bar and Grill.

And then he saw it and his blood that was already thin took on a coolness as well and felt like it had stopped in his veins. He gripped the rim of the Thunderbird's seat, feeling every turn of the tires on the road as the Thunderbird ground to a stop.

'Well,' said Jubal Early, 'I guess this is it.' He was peering through the windshield across the road to the restaurant. 'Sure is a nice place, ain't it?'

But Ethan Pierce was just staring, just feeling the thumping of his heart, just thinking *Oh Jesus Oh Jesus* —

65

THE FOLLOWING, from *Acts Of God* (*How The Lord Shows His Hand*) by Emerson E. Gardner:

> As he [Ethan Pierce] crossed the street on that hot and fateful morning the eyes of the Lord were upon him, and make no mistake readers those eyes are much brighter than the famous eyes of Texas or even the eyes of Nevada if Nevada has eyes that is.

Now while this may very well be true (and there's certainly no way to prove that it isn't), Jubal Early, who was sitting in the Thunderbird across the street watching, saw no evidence of it, although what with his being a confirmed non-believer, seeing evidence of the Eyes of God was just about the last thing you'd expect him to see or anyhow admit to, which he didn't. What he *did* see, however, was the old man crossing the street, but not in a straight line like he was keen to get where he was headed, but more with a kind of sidling action like he was a nervous boy on his first day of school. He looked back every few steps and Jubal Early raised his hand in a wave. The truth be told, Jubal Early was kind of nervous too.

At first the old man veered off towards some trees as if it was suddenly real important he study them, but then after a while of trunk-studying something like courage or fear of failure must have gripped him because he turned around and headed straight — not fast, mind, but straight — for the restaurant, and when he got there he slowed a bit but still kept going until he was right at the door, then pushing on the door, then pausing a moment, then stepping right inside.

What happened next Jubal Early could only guess at, for at that moment a tour bus pulled up outside the restaurant and waited for several minutes while some Japanese tourists fussing with their bags and searching for tickets got on. Jubal Early craned his neck but could see nothing and when at last the bus drew away all there was to see were the people in the restaurant sort of milling about, some staring out blank-faced while others were chattering and pointing, and the old man out on the sidewalk and headed unsteadily his way. The old man was paler than ever now, shuffling careless of the traffic as he crossed the street, then clutching the Thunderbird's hood as he made his way round and in.

'Well?' said Jubal Early. The old man was breathing hard, close to gasping. 'Didya see him, sir?'

Ethan shook his head. 'She fainted,' he managed between gasps.

'Fainted, sir? Who fainted?'

And then so did he – or he would have for sure (he was already halfway there, seeing stars) had Jubal Early not slapped him several times and with sting, bringing water to his eyes and a strange sense of floating.

'Sir?' said Jubal Early. 'Are you hearing me, sir?'

'Where am I?' said Ethan, and then it came back to him: how he'd asked for Vern but Vern wasn't there and then Clare coming through and the look on her face and the strange stiff way she'd crumpled. He stared out at the street, seeing her again falling, hearing again the smashing of plates, and he felt so strange and so weary that he just closed his eyes and all he wanted to do was sleep forever, but Jubal Early slapped again and Ethan sat up, wrenched out of the hands of sleep. He blinked twice – *Where am I?* he thought – stared hard at the pale face before him. 'Who are you?' he said and then it came to him: 'A priest?'

Quick-thinking as ever Jubal Early gave a nod and set upon his face an expression of some gravity. He raised his hand, made the sign of a cross. 'Bless you,' he whispered, drawing up from the soles of his old dusty shoes the most pious and forgiving of smiles.

66

IT WAS WEIRD, but no matter how hard she tried Marla could make no sense of the little man's words. She studied his lips moving behind the microphone as he swayed to and fro with the movement of the bus but all that seemed to come from them was gibberish like he was talking backwards or something just to fool her or was maybe from another planet. She glanced at the man beside her. He was little too and made her feel like some kind of giant, what with his tiny little hands and pitch-black hair that was shiny like it was painted, and when he turned to look at her he was grinning and she saw he had teeth about as tiny and white as a baby's.

'Amelica!' he was saying, grinning harder than ever, until it looked to Marla like his head might split in two. 'I rike Amelica!'

She squinted hard, watching the little man lifting his camera, hearing the click of a shutter release and the whirr of an auto-wind, and all the time she was thinking *What on earth's going on?* For a moment she thought she was maybe on her holidays, heading up to see her brother in Utah, but then she remembered her brother was dead and so she couldn't be and she remembered how she'd tried to figure out where's Da Nang and how she'd looked on a map but she never had found it and how in the end she'd just given up because how would it change things even if she did find it – it wouldn't bring him back, would it?

A light tapping sound drew her back from her memories.

'Neary zere,' said the little man.

'What?' said Marla.

He was tapping on the page of a back-to-front guidebook. 'You rook,' he said grinning, passing it over.

Marla stared at the photo. It was a photo of a dam, blue water, white walls, tiny little cars, even tinier people. She tried to read the writing but the writing was weird. She handed the book back. She seemed to be floating. She stared at the window, her reflection in the glass, and all at once in a rush what had happened returned. There was Perry in the Dairy Queen and then he was gone, Duane too, then the Indian boy driving off into traffic, then a letter from the President and her brother getting killed in some Godawful jungle. Everybody leaving: that was her memory, and now, she remembered, it was time for her too. But she was calm, she wasn't afraid, and when the bus swept a corner into sunshine and there was suddenly clapping and pointing all around her she found herself clapping and pointing too and smiling at the little man who was grinning at her, and when the bus swept down and drew slow into traffic she couldn't help thinking it was drawing her home and that soon there'd be sleeping and peace.

67

WITHOUT A DOUBT Vern Pierce had by far the best pitch —
across the road from the Governor's podium with his back to the
sheer awesome drop of the dam — but that wasn't it, and neither
was the fact that he had the best food — the best burgers and
fries, the best chili dogs; what it was, what accounted for the fact
that since seven o'clock that morning he'd been shifting more
food than he'd ever dreamed possible, was simply having Tuesday
and her smiling standing right there beside him drawing people
from their buses and cars like they had no choice but to get
drawn. Even the Governor, who everyone knew was a man quite
impervious to pretty much everything including sound econom-
ics, just couldn't do anything in the face of such temptation and
when he stepped right over and smiled at Tuesday and ordered
fifteen chili dogs, one for each of his staff, and a burger and fries
for his wife, he surprised a lot of people including himself and
especially his wife who was known for having once flown a chef
all the way from New York just to make the cranberry sauce for
a Thanksgiving dinner. And then when he'd stood and announced
to a gathering of reporters that that chili dog was the best chili
dog he'd ever ever tasted, well, that was it and things had just
gone wild, until now as the sun drifted high towards noon and
the ceremony, and the Governor was shuffling his papers on the
podium, they were all but out of buns and were needing some
more and so Vern slipped away as the Governor started speaking
and made his way through the crowds, not sorry to be leaving
the chaos. His ears were ringing and his feet were pounding. He
just had to get some silence and some rest.

It was cool inside the Visitors' Center and he found himself a
place by some tall plants and sat down. He closed his eyes and

eased off his shoes. From here he could still hear the Governor, but just the fact he was speaking and not what he was saying. The voice was just a drone, and with the fans overhead it was enough to make Vern ease his breathing and drift.

He woke abruptly, squinted at his watch. Only a minute had passed but it felt like an hour. He rubbed his eyes. He sat a moment, then put on his shoes and pushed himself up. He made his way across the floor to the men's room.

It was kind of unnerving but now he was getting older — edging fifty — he was starting to do things he'd never thought he'd do, like napping, for example. Sometimes it seemed like only yesterday he was lying in his room listening to his mama snoozing loud at the TV and thinking she must be about a million years old and how there was no way he was ever gonna do that, but here he was. He studied his face in the mirror. He was forty-eight years old now and sometimes he felt every minute of it. Sometimes it was tough to imagine ever having been a child.

He washed his hands and dried them and made his way back outside. The Governor must have finished speaking as there were people now drifting in out of the sun, looking at the exhibits and clicking their way through the turnstiles to the shop. Vern weaved his way through to the phones.

And sometimes it wasn't just getting old that was scary. Sometimes it was thinking about what he might do. After all, now he was fifty and snoozing like his mama, what's to say he wouldn't turn out like his daddy too? What's to say he wouldn't wake up one morning and feel everything had changed and tell himself and believe it that he had to just get out and go live someplace like Shreveport with some red-headed whore? What's to say there ain't things beyond a man's control, other forces in the universe that have some kind of influence — planets and stuff — and however much you want to fight them you can't fight them and you just wind up doing things you never believed you were ever gonna do? There's nothing to say that — that's what — and sometimes you just gotta think that what people really know don't amount to much and that we're all living blind and that if you get through to the end without some kind of stumbling, well, that's some kind of miracle ain't it?

'Hey, you using that thing?'

Vern looked up from his thinking. He was standing in a phone booth, there were people behind him waiting. He picked up the receiver and put in his money. He dialed the restaurant's number.

'Hello? Is that you Clare?'

There were voices in the restaurant, the clattering of plates.

'Vern?'

'Marianne?'

'Oh, Vern, am I glad you called —'

'What is it, Marianne?'

'It's Clare, Vern —'

Vern Pierce felt a sudden stab of fear. 'What is is?' he said, trying to stay calm.

'Well —'

'I said what is it?'

'Well, she collapsed, Vern —'

'Collapsed?'

'But she's gonna be okay. It was just the shock —'

'What shock?'

'Well —' Marianne paused, there was crackling on the line. 'It was seeing your daddy like that —'

'What?'

'Well, seeing the man who *said* he was your daddy —'

Vern was staring hard at the glass, his mind in a scramble.

'Vern? You still there?'

Yes, he said, he was still there.

'You better come back, Vern.'

He opened his mouth but before he could speak the connection was cut and the coins rattled down through the box. He stood still for a moment, hardly aware of a tapping on the glass.

'Hey, you — are you coming out of there or what?'

He replaced the receiver and stepped out of the booth. *It was seeing your daddy.* He closed his eyes, trying to think.

'Excuse me,' said a voice, 'but are you okay?'

He turned, squinting. 'What?'

231

The woman stepped back as if she'd been slapped. 'I was only asking,' she said, moving away. In a moment she was lost in the crowd.

Some kind of a joke, thought Vern. Had to be. He drew a deep breath but then he thought, *Why?* He made his way through the people to the doors and out. What if there are things a person can't understand? What if the power of wishing and love really can change the world? He was shaky suddenly; he sat down on a wall beside a tree and was just trying to think — just trying to figure things out — when a shriek came up from some way past the podium and then people were running away down the road heading for the dam and Vern was thinking *My God, someone's let off a bomb* and then he was thinking *Jesus Christ, someone's gone and shot the Governor —*

68

WHAT MARLA COULDN'T FIGURE was why all the fuss? It was like what she was doing, standing up there on the ledge halfway across the dam with the road about four foot down one side and the sheer drop of the dam on the other, was suddenly something special and like it was everyone's business, which it was not, instead of just some private thing, which it most certainly was. Heavens, she thought, to look at the people all shrieking and calling and the wailing cars with their flashing lights and the clicking cameras, not to mention the man in the uniform with a cap that had a peak so shiny it could blind a person easing towards her saying, 'Take it easy darlin',' you'd think that they'd never seen a person on a ledge before let alone a person on a ledge getting ready to jump. Which is what she'd do if they'd just let her be, which they didn't seem to want to, especially the man in the cap. 'Now, come on, darlin',' he was saying still, despite her fixing him with a real hard look. 'You don't wanna do this now, do you?'

'Well, yes I do,' said Marla, 'and I'd be obliged if you all would just leave me be.' She scanned the faces below her, their mouths were open and eyes goggling. 'Ain't you people got no places to go?'

'Hey, darlin',' said peaked cap, 'what's your name?' He was still easing forward but he stopped this time when she frowned at him.

'Why're you asking that?' she said.

Peaked cap smiled. 'Being friendly, is all.'

'Well, don't,' said Marla. 'I ain't got no time for that.' She looked over the ledge; breath was drawn in the crowd. To Marla it looked like a million miles down but not scary any more for all that. Oh sure, she'd been scared for a minute or two, but not any more. She was kind of used to it by now. She looked back at peaked cap. He was talking now to a man in a sandy-colored suit, pointing towards her and shrugging his shoulders. In a moment the man in the sandy-colored suit broke away and edged across the road towards her.

'Hi there,' he said. He was smiling like he'd just won some Biggest Smile competition. 'My name's Mr McCarthur, but you can call me Cormac. I'm the Governor of this here fine state.' He paused, still smiling. 'And you are?'

'Well if *you're* the Governor then I guess that means I *ain't*,' said Marla who was getting real weary of it all. Didn't they have no discretion? Couldn't they figure that jumping from a dam is a private kind of thing? 'Look,' she said, 'I got business here – personal business – can't y'all see that?'

'Sure,' said the Governor. He was grinning even harder than before now. 'We're just trying to help, is all.'

'You want to help?' said Marla. 'I'll tell you how you can help. By turning around – all of you.'

For a moment the Governor's smile took a dip. 'Turn around?' he said. 'Why?'

'Privacy – that's why.'

But then the smile was back up to full power. 'Look –' he said.

'I mean it,' said Marla.

'Okay,' said the Governor. He turned away and then one by one the crowd turned too. The last to turn was a TV crew.

'Thank you,' said Marla. She stood gazing at the backs of heads for a moment thinking maybe she should say something, but then she thought *Why should I?* and she eased herself around on the ledge. She looked down. The water below was distant and blue and she could smell it and it smelled so sweet and was beckoning. She closed her eyes and raised her arms like a diver and pointed her toes. 'Here I come,' she whispered, pushing off.

But then something happened or rather didn't, because when she'd planned to be sailing on down towards oblivion she wasn't, and so she opened her eyes and looked down at her legs

234

accusingly but her legs wouldn't move. She squinted in the light. There were arms wrapped around her and a face looking up.

'Well, howdee,' said Jubal Early.

'Perry?' said Marla.

'Pardon me?'

And then she saw Ethan, he was smiling a ways off then tumbling to the ground, and then there were voices and wailing cars and then folks running this way and that and then a strange shifting feeling and then blackness, then nothing.

Six

69

'I SWEAR IT!' said Virginia. She was down on her knees in the Brinkman house parlor, staring hard at the TV's murky flickering. 'I saw him!'

Dorothy sat heavily on the arm of a chair. She'd been out in the yard feeding the chickens and still had the bowl in her hands. She peered at the TV. 'Are you sure?' she said.

'Positive,' said Virginia.

'You actually saw him?'

Virginia turned sharply. 'I said so, didn't I?'

Dorothy shrugged. She felt suddenly exhausted. She'd had a feeling all morning something like this was going to happen, and so had the chickens. They'd been rattling the mesh of their run since daybreak. 'You could have made a mistake,' she said. 'The picture's awful grainy —'

Virginia sighed. 'I told you I saw him, so I saw him — alright? It was right after that woman jumped off —'

'Jumped off?' Dorothy felt a shock like a slap.

'Well, tried to, anyhow,' said Virginia, looking back now at the TV. It had once been black and white but was now mostly grey; it was like watching things happening through a glass of dirty water. 'She was standing on some ledge getting ready to dive when this man just turned up and grabbed her —'

'What man?'

She shrugged. 'I don't know, do I? Just some man. Kinda weird-looking, though. Had this real long coat and his face was real white. Hey look!'

Dorothy jumped. 'What?'

On the screen through the murk a body was being carried on a stretcher towards a waiting ambulance.

'That's him!'

Dorothy stared hard and sure enough there he was, Ethan on the stretcher, his face just as white as the TV could make it. 'Is he dead?' she asked. Her heart was thumping.

Virginia shrugged. 'You mean *again?*' she said, and just as she said it the front door opened and banged shut and then Frank Tyler was standing in his overalls in the doorway, his chest pumping hard like he'd been running. 'Jesus,' he managed between gasps. 'You see that?' and he stared at Dorothy who was staring at the floor. 'Dorothy?'

'She saw it,' said Virginia. On the screen through the murk now a man in a sandy-colored suit was shaking his head and smiling. *A miracle*, he was saying and then *Critically ill*, and then he was gone and in his place came a woman selling shoes.

70

THEY WERE SITTING silent round the table in the kitchen when the first call came. For a moment no one moved, like they were all too heavy with their thinking to move, but then Frank pushed himself up and crossed the room.

'Yes?'

'Who is it?' said Virginia, but Frank waved her be quiet, and then he just stood there listening, sometimes saying *Yep* or *Nope* but never saying more. Finally he put down the phone. He hadn't said goodbye.

'Well?' said Virginia.

Frank sat down. He had that sort of pinched look on his face he got when he was thinking.

'Who was it, Frank?' said Dorothy. 'Was it the hospital?'

Frank shook his head. 'He ain't in a hospital, Dorothy. He's lying upstairs above some restaurant —'

'A restaurant?' said Virginia. 'What the hell's he doing in a restaurant?'

'I said *above a* restaurant, Ginny.'

'Is it Vern's?' said Dorothy.

Frank nodded. 'That was some paper out west,' he said. 'Say they're looking for details.'

'What details?'

'About Ethan mostly, background and stuff, they say they wanna pay —'

Virginia looked up. 'Pay?' she said. 'Did they say how much?'

Frank shook his head. He looked gravely at Dorothy. 'They say he's dying, Dorothy.' He reached for her hand, enclosed it. 'You want to go see him?'

'You bet!' said Virginia, but Dorothy shook her head.

'You sure?'

She nodded.

'Why not?' said Virginia, but her sister just got up and walked slow across the room. There were footsteps on the stairs then the closing of a door.

She was lying on her bed when Frank tapped on the door and eased it open. 'Dorothy?' he whispered. 'You okay?' She was lying on her side, her face towards the window. She'd been crying.

Frank stepped in and closed the door behind him. He crossed to the bed and sat down.

Dorothy turned. 'Frank?' she whispered.

'I'm here.'

'Has he gone yet?'

'I don't know,' said Frank and it was true: after the first five or so calls he'd just let the phone ring. It was ringing now. It stopped.

'Do you think it'll be long?'

He shrugged. 'I guess not.' He paused. There was something on his mind.

Dorothy shifted on the bed. 'What is it, Frank?'

He looked down at his hands. 'Can I ask you something?' he said.

'Of course.'

He looked up. 'Something personal?'

'I guess. What is it?'

'Well –' He paused again.

'Frank?'

He was biting his lip. 'Well, did you love him – Ethan, I mean?'

'Yes I did,' said Dorothy. 'Why?'

'Well, it's just I was thinking, about Ethan coming back and all –'

'What about it?'

'Well I was thinking that, well, maybe that's *why* he came back –'

242

Dorothy pushed herself up. She was frowning. 'What are you saying?'

'Well, don't you see? Maybe it was you that brought him back, maybe he knew how much you loved him and he just couldn't die, but then things just got screwed up somehow and he wound up in Boulder –' Frank paused, he was breathing hard, searching Dorothy's face for confirmation. 'Well, don't you think?' he said.

Dorothy shook her head. 'You know what I think?' she said softly. 'I think you're right but you got the wrong person. I think it was Vern that made him come back not me. That's why he's in Boulder and not here.'

There were footsteps on the stairs.

'Frank?'

Frank looked up. Dorothy was smiling. 'What is it?' he said. 'Why're you smiling?'

'I'm smiling 'cause of you, Frank.'

'Why?'

Dorothy took his hand and covered it. 'Because you're such a good man, that's why, and you know what?'

'What?'

But she never got to say what because just at that moment the door was flung open and Virginia stepped in, unsteady on her legs, a bottle of Judge Brinkman's finest brandy in her hand.

'Virginia?' said Dorothy. 'Have you been drinking?'

Virginia smiled and stepped back against the doorframe. 'Sister, we're rich!' she said, her words tripping into each other. 'I just done us a deal that means millions!'

'A deal?' said Frank.

Virginia shrugged, raising the bottle. 'Well thousands, anyhow,' she said. 'And that ain't all –'

'Oh, Ginny,' sighed Dorothy.

But before Virginia could mention movie rights and Ann-Margaret she was sliding down the wall and then resting in a heap, a smile on her face and her dress up around her thighs and her tennis shoes splayed, laces as ever untied, one shoe pointing east and the other pointing west.

'Well,' said Dorothy.

'Well,' said Frank.

'You know what?'

'What?'

But then they were laughing and no more was said, and when the telephone rang they just let it ring and ring, and when the morning slipped away they just sat in silence in the old Brinkman house, the three of them together as ever they would be, together but thinking their own separate thoughts.

71

ETHAN DRIFTED IN and out all afternoon like a radio signal in a
storm, one minute he was awake and rambling and the next he
was so still Vern thought he was dead. Every now and then Vern
got up and crossed the room and looked out of the window but
every time there were just more people in the street looking up.
Sometimes they waved but he didn't wave back, and when it
started getting dark he just closed the curtains. At three Clare
came in with some soup saying *You've got to eat something* but
he didn't feel like eating, it didn't seem right somehow. So he just
left the soup to cool on the table and went on watching and
waiting, but for what he couldn't say.

From the start he'd had this one thought: maybe he'll wake up
and then he'll explain and everything won't seem so weird like
he was in a dream, but every time he looked like he was going to
wake up, every time he started talking, every time he opened his
eyes, his lips would freeze and his eyes drop closed again and
he'd drift back to emptiness or sleep or someplace so far away
you could shout and he still wouldn't hear you. And every time
he was gone again Vern would start thinking *Well, maybe that's it*,
that maybe his father never would explain, never say what had
happened or why he'd done what he'd done, and that maybe it
was all just part of some plan, and then he'd start thinking about
God and wondering if God really was so damn brilliant in the
way He arranges things or whether He was just real mean. And
then he'd start feeling guilty, of course, and think maybe he
should pray just in case, but the two times he actually got down
on his knees he couldn't think of anything to say except *Please
wake him up* which just sounded so selfish and not what praying
is supposed to be about, so he'd just given up and gone back to

staring and every now and then getting up and looking out the window, down at the people with their cameras and leather-backed notebooks, all the time thinking as he watched them waving how they looked like those people you see on the news standing around outside a prison just waiting for the drop. And then he'd get to thinking *Well isn't that what I'm doing?* which of course he was not. He was waiting for life not death, because only through the living are things ever made clear. Things like whores and running off to Shreveport, like leaving a family For No Good Reason, not to mention other things like a person who's dead suddenly coming back to life and how can this happen and if it did why now?

Vern stared at his father but his father wasn't saying. His father was sleeping and dying. Maybe dead, he thought suddenly, and he leaned over the bed and put his ear to the old man's chest. There was a heartbeat but distant like the beat of a drum through a wall, but at least there was a heartbeat and he wasn't dead yet. There was still time. Vern sat back, took his father's hand in his. He closed his eyes.

'Vern?'

He woke with a start. It was Clare. He sat up. 'What is it?' he said. He stared at his father. 'Is he dead?'

'No,' said Clare, 'he's sleeping. How about you? Are you okay?'

'I'm fine,' said Vern.

'Sure now?'

'Sure.'

And then Clare was gone and Vern stood up, tried to stretch out the tiredness from his limbs. He crossed to the window and peeked out. Down below in the street the reporters were still there. They were standing around kicking cans, the red of their cigarettes glowing in the dark. He watched them for a while (they couldn't see him any more, or didn't want to) and then he went back to his chair by the bed. He listened to his father's steady shallow breathing. He was aware of time ticking by.

Looking back on it now it seemed a strange thing, but when he'd broken through the crowds and seen his father lying on his back on the road and all the people around him – the paramedics and cops, the Governor giving interviews and smiling – it was almost as if he'd known he'd be there, as if he'd expected it, and he'd not felt surprise so much as a sudden intense relief. It was like suddenly all those years he'd been waiting hadn't been wasted after all and the faith that had seemed so ridiculous even to him and real hard sometimes to sustain wasn't just hopeless and he wasn't just blind and it meant too that maybe there's nothing that cannot be reversed through faith, no situation so bad that it's too bad to get turned around. But it meant most of all that the precious circle of family need not be broken, that hands once withdrawn still can find other hands, that a person cast adrift really can find the shore.

He was down the hall in the bathroom when his father coughed and woke for the last time. 'Dad?' he called out, he was racing down the hall. He crossed the dark room, leaned over the bed. He was panting, still clutching a towel. 'Dad? Are you okay?' His father's face was deathly pale, his eyes wide but blind.

'Vern?' he whispered, a rasp in his throat.

Vern nodded. 'It's me, Dad. Can you hear me?'

For a moment Ethan was silent, just breathing, then he said, 'Is Clare there?'

'No, Dad,' said Vern. 'Should I get her?'

Ethan moved his head, *No.*

'Then I'll get the doctor –'

Again, *No.*

'But he's only a block away –'

Another twist of the head. Ethan drew a shallow breath. 'Vern?'

Vern leaned closer, he could feel the faint touch of his father's breath. 'What is it, Dad?'

Ethan drew another breath. 'Bulb,' he whispered, turning his head, nodding towards the bedside lamp.

'You want the lightbulb?' said Vern.

Ethan nodded, flexed the fingers of his right hand, and when his fingers found the shaft of the bulb they gripped it and then faintly the bulb began to glow, flickering at first but then steady, casting a low yellow light across the bed. 'Lightning,' he whispered.

Vern was staring at the bulb, then staring at his father. 'Jesus,' he said. 'You mean —'

'Lightning,' said Ethan again. He closed his eyes a second; the bulb flickered. Then he was squinting, trying hard, the effort of speech exhausting. 'Vern?' he whispered.

'It's okay, Dad.'

But he turned his head, *No*: there were things to say that he had to get said. He moved his lips: *Forgive me.*

'There's nothing to forgive,' said Vern, though he knew this wasn't so. There were years and absence and more.

Another turn, left, right: *Yes there is.*

Vern took the old man's free hand in his. He held it tight. 'I love you, Dad,' he said. 'What's gone is gone.'

Ethan raised his brows, doubting.

Vern looked away, then back. 'Dad?'

'Yes?' A whisper: the old man was sounding more distant now.

'Why did you go?'

Suddenly there were tears in Ethan's blind eyes. He was thinking of a home, of a family, of the years.

'Didn't you love us?' said Vern, but even as he said it he knew the answer.

Ethan Pierce turned his head a last time on the pillow. He drew a last breath. 'I loved you,' he whispered, then his hand moved in fear. 'Vern?'

'I'm here, Dad.'

'Vern?'

Then the bulb flickered rapidly for a moment, then slowed in its flickering and was gone and the room passed again into darkness.

'Dad?' said Vern. He laid his head on his father's chest, listening, but his father was still. He closed his eyes. There was nothing to hear now but the regular sound of his own heart beating and the murmur of voices through the wall.

*

248

It was nearing dawn when Clare Pierce found her husband. He was sitting on the wall halfway across the dam looking out across the water to the mountains and the sky. She moved up beside him and leaned against the wall. 'He's gone then,' she said softly.

Vern nodded. He opened his mouth to speak but something stopped him. Being there and never leaving was enough, all that mattered. He put his arm around his wife and drew her to him and together they watched as the western sun rose, watched its light spilling over the water and the land, heard the sounds of the awakening desert.

72

FROM THE *Boulder City Clarion*, June 21st 1994:

WAITRESS TO WED

The engagement was announced today of Miss Marla Thomson, newest employee of Vern's Bar and Grill on Main Street, to Mr Rod Mickelsson of Mickelsson's Mufflers, Las Vegas. It is understood by this paper that neither the bride nor the groom wish a great fuss to be made of their forthcoming nuptials, a request to which the *Boulder City Clarion* is happy to accede.

From *Weird But True Magazine*, March 1995:

CUSTER ALIVE!

Reports are coming in from Our Man Jubal A. Early, that General George Armstrong Custer, scourge of the Sioux, is alive and living in the state of Oklahoma. At one hundred and sixty-five years of age, the General, though confined now to a saddle-mounted wheelchair, has it appears lost none of his famous fighting spirit – as his neighbor Sitting Bull confirms. 'He's nuts!' the wiley old Redskin told Our Man – and not, it seems, without reason, for shortly thereafter a missile was thrown and Our Man was forced to retreat to the safety of a nearby tree, from where he filed this extraordinary report.

From the *Bagdad Bugle*, June 2nd 1996:

ETHAN PIERCE HONORED

It now being two years Monday since the passing of Ethan Pierce, famously known from the movie as the Lightning Man, a service of Thanksgiving is to be held at three o'clock at the

First Baptist Church of Bagdad. Following the service, refreshments will be provided (for which thanks go to Wal-Mart and Mr Frank Tyler, Manager) in the Judge Brinkman Suite at the Bagdad Best Western, where at five o'clock promptly Governor Jackson will say a few words. It is hoped that the Governor will be taking this opportunity to formally announce the creation of Ethan Pierce County, said county thus becoming the sixteenth and newest county within the borders of the glorious state of Arizona.